# "The Wall of Storm

confronts the Wall of Dark; the Narrow Land extends—how far? Who knows? If to infinity then
all possibilities must be realized; then there are
other Ones, Twos and Threes. If the Narrow Land
terminates at Chaos, then we may be alone."

"I have travelled sea-right and sea-left until
wide rivers stopped me," said Ern. "The Narrow
Land continued without any sign of coming to an
end. I believe that it must extend to infinity; in
fact, it is hard to conceive of a different situation. . . ."

# THE
# NARROW
# LAND

*Jack Vance*

**D A W   B o o k s ,   I n c .**
Donald A. Wollheim, Publisher
1633 Broadway, New York, N.Y. 10019

PUBLISHED BY
THE NEW AMERICAN LIBRARY
OF CANADA LIMITED

ACKNOWLEDGMENTS

*The Narrow Land,* © 1967 by Ultimate Pub. Co. *The Masquerade on Dicantropus,* © 1951 by Standard Magazines, Inc. *Where Hesperus Falls,* © 1956 by King-Size Pubs., Inc. *The World-Thinker,* © 1945, by Standard Magazines, Inc. *Green Magic,* © 1963 by Mercury Press, Inc. *The Ten Books,* © 1951 by Standard Magazines, Inc. *Chateau D'If,* © 1950 by Standard Magazines, Inc. as *New Bodies for Old.*

FIRST PRINTING, JULY 1982

2 3 4 5 6 7 8 9

 DAW TRADEMARK REGISTERED
U.S. PAT. OFF. MARCA REGISTRADA.
HECHO EN WINNIPEG, CANADA

PRINTED IN CANADA
COVER PRINTED IN U.S.A.

# Table of Contents

# Table of Contents

# The Narrow Land

A pair of nerves joined across the top of Ern's brain; he became conscious, aware of darkness and constriction. The sensation was uncomfortable. He tensed his members, thrust at the shell, meeting resistance in all directions except one. He kicked, butted and presently created a rupture. The constriction eased somewhat. Ern squirmed around, clawed at the membrane, tore it back and was met by a sudden unpleasant exudation: the juices of a being not himself. It wrenched around, reached forth. Ern recoiled, struck back the probing members, which seemed ominously strong and massive.

There was a period of passivity. Each found the other hateful: they were of the same sort, yet different. Presently the two small creatures fought, with little near-inaudible squeaks and chitters.

Ern eventually strangled his opponent. When he tried to detach himself, he found that an adhesion of tissue had occurred, that the two were now one. Ern expanded himself, rounded and fused with the defeated individual.

For a further period Ern rested, exploring his consciousness. The constriction once again became oppressive. Ern thrust and kicked, creating a new rupture, and the shell split wide.

Ern struggled forth into soft slime, then up into a glare of light, an acrid dry void. From above came a harsh cry. An enormous shape hurtled down. Ern dodged, evaded a pair of clicking black prongs. He flapped, paddled, slid down into cool water, where he submerged himself.

Others inhabited the water; Ern saw their dim shapes to all sides. Some were like himself: pale pop-eyed sprats, narrow-skulled with wisps of film for crests. Others were larger, with the legs and arms definitely articulated, the crests stiffer, the skin tough and silver-gray. Ern bestirred himself, tested his arms and legs. He swam, carefully at first, then with competence. Hunger came; he ate: larvae, nodules on the roots of reeds, trifles of this and that.

So Ern entered his childhood, and gradually became wise in the ways of the waterworld. Duration could not be measured; there was no basis for time: no alteration of light and darkness, no change except for Ern's own growth. The only notable events of the sea-shallows were tragedies. A water-baby frolicking too far, recklessly, offshore might be caught in a current and swept out under the storm-curtain. The armored birds from time to time carried away a very young baby basking at the surface. Most dreadful of all was the ogre who lived in one of the sea-sloughs: a brutish creature with long arms, a flat face and four bony ridges over the top of its skull. On one occasion Ern almost became its victim. Skulking under the roots of the swamp-reeds, the ogre lunged forth; Ern felt the swirl of water and darted away, the ogre's grasp so near that the claws scraped his leg. The ogre pursued, making idiotic sounds, then, jerking aside, seized one of Ern's playfellows, and settled to the bottom to munch upon its captive.

After Ern grew large enough to defy the predator birds, he spent much time on the surface, tasting the air and marveling at the largeness of the vistas, though he understood nothing of what he saw. The sky was a dull gray fog, somewhat brighter out over the sea, never changing except for an occasional wind-whipped cloud or a trail of rain. Close at hand was the swamp: sloughs, low-lying islands overgrown with pallid reeds, complicated black shrubs of the utmost fragility, a few spindly dendrons. Beyond hung a wall of black murk. On the seaward side the horizon was obscured by a lightning-shattered wall of cloud and rain. The wall of murk and the wall of storm ran parallel, delineating the borders of the region between.

The larger of the water-children tended to congregate at the surface. There were two sorts. The typical individual was slender and lithe, with a narrow bony skull, a single crest, protuberant eyes. His temperament was mercurial; he tended to undignified wrangling and sudden brisk fights which were over almost as soon as they started. The sex differences were definite: some were male, half as many were female.

In contrast, and much in the minority, were the twin-crested water-children. These were more massive, with broader skulls, less prominent eyes and a more sedate disposition. Their sexual differentiation was not obvious, and they regarded the antics of the single-crested children with disapproval.

Ern identified himself with this latter group though his crest development was not yet definite, and, if anything, he was even broader and more stocky than the others. Sexually he was slow in developing, but he seemed definitely masculine.

The oldest of the children, single- and double-crested alike, knew a few elements of speech, passed down the classes from a time and source unknown. In due course Ern learned the language, and thereafter idled away long periods discussing the events of the sea-shallows. The wall of storm with its incessant dazzle of lightning was continually fascinating, but the children gave most of their attention to the swamp and rising ground beyond, where, by virtue of tradition transmitted along with the language, they knew their destiny lay, among the "men."

Occasionally "men" would be seen probing the shore mud for flatfish, or moving among the reeds on mysterious errands. At such times the water-children, impelled by some unknown emotion, would instantly submerge themselves, all except the most daring of the single-crested who would float with only their eyes above water, to watch the men at their fascinating activities.

Each appearance of the men stimulated discussion among the water-children. The single-crested maintained that all would become men and walk the dry land, which they declared to be a condition of bliss. The double-crested, more skeptical, agreed that the children might go ashore—after all, this was the tradition—but what next? Tradition offered no information on this score, and the discussions remained speculative.

At long last Ern saw men close at hand. Searching the bottom for crustaceans, he heard a strong rhythmic splashing and, looking up, saw three large long figures: magnificent creatures! They swam with power and grace; even the ogre might avoid such as these! Ern followed at a discreet distance wondering if he dared approach and make himself known. It would be pleasant, he thought, to talk with these men, to learn about life on the shore . . . The men paused to inspect a school of playing children, pointing here and there, while the children halted their play to stare up in wonder. Now occurred a shocking incident. The largest of the double-crested water-children was Zim the Name-giver, a creature, by Ern's reckoning, old and wise. It was Zim's prerogative to ordain names for his fellows: Ern had received his name from Zim. It now chanced that Zim, unaware of the men, wandered into view. The men pointed, uttered sharp guttural cries and plunged below the surface. Zim, startled into immobility, hesitated an instant, then darted away. The men pursued, harrying him this way and that, apparently intent on his capture. Zim, wild with fear, swam far offshore, out over the gulf, where the current took him and carried him away, out toward the curtain of storm.

The men, exclaiming in anger, plunged landward in foaming strokes of arms and legs.

In fascinated curiosity Ern followed: up a large slough, finally to a beach of packed mud. The men waded ashore, strode off among the reeds. Ern drifted slowly forward, beset by a quivering conflict of impulses. How, he wondered, could beings so magnificent hound Zim the Name-giver to his doom? The land was close; the footprints of the men were plain on the mud of the beach; where did they lead? What wonderful new vistas lay beyond the line of reeds? Ern eased forward to the beach. He lowered his feet and tried to walk. His legs felt limp and flexible; only by dint of great concentration was he able to set one foot before the other. Deprived of the support of the water his body felt gross and clumsy. From the reeds came a screech of amazement. Ern's legs, suddenly capable, carried him in wobbling leaps down the beach. He plunged into the water, swam frantically back along the slough. Behind him came men, churning the water. Ern ducked aside, hid behind a clump of rotting reeds. The men continued down the slough, out over the shallows where they spent a fruitless period ranging back and forth.

Ern remained in his cover. The men returned, passing no more than the length of their bodies from Ern's hiding place, so close that he could see their glittering eyes and the dark yellow interior of their oral cavities when they gasped for air. With their spare frames, prow-shaped skulls and single crests they resembled neither Ern nor Zim, but rather the single-crested water-children. These were not his sort! He was not a man! Perplexed, seething with excitement and dissatisfaction, Ern returned to the shallows.

But nothing was as before. The innocence of the easy old life had departed; there was now a portent in the air which soured the pleasant old routines. Ern found it hard to wrench his attention away from the shore and he considered the single-crested children, his erstwhile playmates, with new wariness: they suddenly seemed strange, different from himself, and they in turn watched the double-crested children with distrust, swimming away in startled shoals when Ern or one of the others came by.

Ern became morose and dour. The old satisfactions were gone; there were no compensations. Twice again the men swam out across the shallows, but all the double-crested children, Ern among them, hid under reeds. The men thereupon appeared to lose interest, and for a period life went on more or less as before. But change was in the wind. The shoreline became a preoccupation: what lay behind the reed islands, between the reed islands and the wall of murk? Where did the men live, in what wonderful surroundings? With the most extreme vigilance against the ogre Ern swam up the largest of the sloughs. To either side were islands overgrown with pale reeds, with an occasional black skeleton-tree or a globe of tangle bush: stuff so fragile as to collapse at a touch. The slough branched, opening into still coves reflecting the gray gloom of the sky, and at last narrowed, dwindling to a channel of black slime.

Ern dared proceed no farther. If someone or something had followed him, he was trapped. And at this moment a strange yellow creature halted overhead to hover on a thousand tinkling scales. Spying Ern it set up a wild ululation. Off in the distance Ern thought to hear a call of harsh voices: men. He swung around and swam back the way he had come, with the tinkle-bird careening above. Ern ducked under the surface, swam down the slough at full speed. Presently he went to the side, cautiously surfaced. The yellow bird swung in erratic circles over the point where he had submerged, its quavering howl now diminished to a mournful hooting sound.

Ern gratefully returned to the shallows. It was now clear to him that if ever he wished to go ashore he must learn to walk. To the perplexity of his fellows, even those of the double-crests, he began to clamber up through the mud of the near island, exercising his legs among the reeds. All went passably well, and Ern presently found himself walking without effort though as yet he dared not try the land behind the islands. Instead he swam along the coast, the storm-wall on his right hand, the shore on his left. On and on he went, farther than he had ever ventured before.

The storm-wall was changeless: a roll of rain and a thick

vapor lanced with lightning. The wall of murk was the same:
dense black at the horizon, lightening by imperceptible grada-
tions to become the normal gloom of the sky overhead.
The narrow land extended endlessly onward. Ern saw new
swamps, reed islands; shelves of muddy foreshore, a spit of
sharp rocks. At length the shore curved away, retreated
toward the wall of murk, to form a funnel-shaped bay, into
which poured a freezingly cold river. Ern swam to the shore,
crawled up on the shingle, stood swaying on his still uncer-
tain legs. Far across the bay new swamps and islands continued to the verge of vision and beyond. There was no living
creature in sight. Ern stood alone on the gravel bar, a small
gray figure, swaying on still limber legs, peering earnestly this
way and that. The river curved away and out of sight into
the darkness. The water of the estuary was bitterly cold, the
current ran swift; Ern decided to go no farther. He slipped
into the sea and returned the way he had come.

Back in the familiar shallows he took up his old routine
searching the bottom for crustaceans, taunting the ogre,
floating on the surface with a wary eye for men, testing his
legs on the island. During one of the visits ashore he came
upon a most unusual sight: a woman depositing eggs in the
mud. From behind a curtain of reeds Ern watched in fascination. The woman was not quite so large as the men and
lacked the harsh male facial structure, though her cranial
ridge was no less prominent. She wore a shawl of a dark red
woven stuff: the first garment Ern had ever seen, and he marveled at the urbanity of the men's way of life.

The woman was busy for some time. When she departed,
Ern went to examine the eggs. They had been carefully protected from armored birds by a layer of mud and a neat little
tent of plaited reeds. The nest contained three clutches, each
a row of three eggs, each egg carefully separated from the
next by a wad of mud.

So here, thought Ern, was the origin of the water-babies.
He recalled the circumstances of his own birth; evidently he
had emerged from just such an egg. Rearranging mud and
tent, Ern left the eggs as he had found them and returned to
the water.

Time passed. The men came no more. Ern wondered that
they should abandon an occupation in which they had
showed so vigorous an interest; but then the whole matter
exceeded the limits of his understanding.

He became prey to restlessness once again. In this regard

he seemed unique: none of his fellows had ever wandered beyond the shallows. Ern set off along the shore, this time swimming with the stormwall to his left. He crossed the slough in which lived the ogre, who glared up as Ern passed and made a threatening gesture. Ern swam hastily on, though now he was of a size larger than that which the ogre preferred to attack.

The shore on this side of the shallows was more interesting and varied than that to the other. He came upon three high islands crowned with a varied vegetation—black skeleton trees; stalks with bundles of pink and white foliage clenched in black fingers; glossy lamellar pillars, the topmost scales billowing out into gray leaves—then the islands were no more, and the mainland rose directly from the sea. Ern swam close to the beach to avoid the currents, and presently came to a spit of shingle pushing out into the sea. He climbed ashore and surveyed the landscape. The ground slanted up under a cover of umbrella trees, then rose sharply to become a rocky bluff crested with black and gray vegetation: the most notable sight of Ern's experience.

Ern slid back into the sea, swam on. The landscape slackened, became flat and swampy. He swam past a bank of black slime overgrown with squirming yellow-green fibrils, which he took care to avoid. Some time later he heard a thrashing hissing sound and looking to sea observed an enormous white worm sliding through the water. Ern floated quietly and the worm slid on past and away. Ern continued. On and on he swam until, as before, the shore was broken by an estuary leading away into the murk. Wading up the beach, Ern looked far and wide across a dismal landscape supporting only tatters of brown lichen. The river which flooded the estuary seemed even larger and swifter than the one he had seen previously, and carried an occasional chunk of ice. A bitter wind blew toward the stormwall, creating a field of retreating white-caps. The opposite shore, barely visible, showed no relief or contrast. There was no apparent termination to the narrow land; it appeared to reach forever between the walls of storm and gloom.

Erb returned to the shallows, not wholly satisfied with what he had learned. He had seen marvels unknown to his fellows, but what had they taught him? Nothing. His questions remained unanswered.

Changes were taking place; they could not be ignored. The whole of Ern's class lived at the surface, breathing air. Infected by some pale dilution of Ern's curiosity, they stared uneasily landward. Sexual differentiation was evident; there were tendencies toward sexual play, from which the double-crested children, with undeveloped organs, stood contemptuously aloof. Social as well as physical distinctions developed; there began to be an interchange of taunts and derogation, occasionally a brief skirmish. Ern ranged himself with the double-crested children, although on exploring his own scalp, he found only indecisive hummocks and hollows, which to some extent embarrassed him.

In spite of the general sense of imminence, the coming of the men took the children by surprise.

In the number of two hundred the men came down the sloughs and swam out to surround the shallows. Ern and a few others instantly clambered up among the reeds of the island and concealed themselves. The other children milled and swam in excited circles. The men shouted, slapped the water with their arms; diving and veering, they herded the water-children up the slough, all the way to the beach of dried mud. Here they chose and sorted, sending the largest up the beach, allowing the fingerlings and sprats to return to the shallows, taking the double-crested children with sharp cries of exultation.

The selection was complete. The captive children were marshaled into groups and sent staggering up the trail; those with legs still soft were carried.

Ern, fascinated by the process, watched from a discreet distance. When men and children had disappeared, he emerged from the water, clambered up the beach to look after his departed friends. What to do now? Return to the shallows? The old life seemed drab and insipid. He dared not present himself to the men. They were single-crested; they were harsh and abrupt. What remained? He looked back and forth, between water and land, and at last gave his youth a melancholy farewell: henceforth he would live ashore.

He walked a few steps up the path, stopped to listen.

Silence.

He proceeded warily, prepared to duck into the undergrowth at a sound. The soil underfoot became less sodden; the reeds disappeared and aromatic black cycads lined the path. Above rose slender supple withes, with gas-filled leaves half-floating, half-supported. Ern moved ever more cautiously, pausing to listen ever more frequently. What if he met the men? Would they kill him? Ern hesitated and even looked back along the path . . . The decision had been made. He continued forward.

A sound, from somewhere not too far ahead. Ern dodged off the path, flattened himself behind a hummock.

No one appeared. Ern moved forward through the cycads and, presently, through the black fronds, he saw the village of the men: a marvel of ingenuity and complication! Nearby stood tall bins containing food-stuffs, then, at a little distance, a row of thatched stalls stacked with poles, coils of rope, pots of pigment and grease. Yellow tinkle-birds, perched on the gables, made a constant chuckling clamor. The bins and stalls faced an open space surrounding a large platform, where a ceremony of obvious import was in progress. On the platform stood four men, draped in bands of woven leaves and four women wearing dark red shawls and tall hats decorated with tinkle-bird scales. Beside the platform, in a miserable gray clot, huddled the single-crested children, the individuals distinguishable only by an occasional gleam of eye or twitch of pointed crest.

One by one the children were lifted up to the four men, who gave each a careful examination. Most of the male children were dismissed and sent down into the crowd. The rejects, about one in every ten, were killed by the blow of a stone mallet and propped up to face the wall of storm. The girl-children were sent to the other end of the platform, where the four women waited. Each of the trembling girl-children was considered in turn. About half were discharged from the platform into the custody of a woman and taken to a booth; about one in every five was daubed along the skull with white paint and sent to a nearby pen where the double-crested children were also confined. The rest suffered a blow of the mallet. The corpses were propped to face the wall of murk . . .

Above Ern's head sounded the mindless howl of a tinkle-bird. Ern darted back into the brush. The bird drifted overhead on clashing scales. Men ran to either side, chased Ern back and forth, and finally captured him. He was dragged to the village, thrust triumphantly up on the platform, amid calls of surprise and excitement. The four priests, or whatever their function, surrounded Ern to make their examination. There was a new set of startled outcries. The priests stood back in perplexity, then after a mumble of discussion signaled to the priest-women. The mallet was brought forward—but was never raised. A man from the crowd jumped up on the platform, to argue with the priests. They made a second careful study of Ern's head, muttering to each other. Then one brought a knife, another clamped Ern's head. The knife was drawn the length of his cranium, first to the left of the central ridge, then to the right, to produce a pair of near-parallel cuts. Orange blood trickled down Ern's face; pain made him tense and stiff. A woman brought forward a handful of some vile substance which she rubbed into the wounds. Then all stood away, murmuring and speculating. Ern glared back, half-mad with fear and pain.

He was led to a booth, thrust within. Bars were dropped across the aperture and laced with thongs.

Ern watched the remainder of the ceremony. The corpses were dismembered, boiled and eaten. The white-daubed girl-children were marshaled into a group with all those double-crested children with whom Ern had previously identified himself. Why, he wondered, had he not been included in this group? Why had he first been threatened with the mallet, then wounded with a knife? The situation was incomprehensible.

The girls and the two-crested children were marched away through the brush. The other girls with no more ado became members of the community. The male children underwent a much more formal instruction. Each man took one of the boys under his sponsorship, and subjected him to a rigorous discipline. There were lessons in deportment, knot-tying, weaponry, language, dancing, the various outcries.

Ern received minimal attention. He was fed irregularly, as occasion seemed to warrant. The period of his confinement could not be defined, the changeless gray sky providing no chronometric reference; and indeed, the concept of time as a succession of definite interims was foreign to Ern's mind. He escaped apathy only by attending the instruction in adjoining booths, where single-crested boys were taught language and deportment. Ern learned the language long before those under instruction; he and his double-crested fellows had used the rudiments of this language in the long-gone halcyon past.

The twin wounds along Ern's skull eventually healed, leaving parallel weals of scar-tissue. The black feathery combs of maturity were likewise sprouting, covering his entire scalp with down.

None of his erstwhile comrades paid him any heed. They had become indoctrinated in the habits of the village; the old life of the shallows had receded in their memories. Watching

them stride past his prison, Ern found them increasingly
apart from himself. They were lithe, slender, agile, like tall
keen-featured lizards. He was heavier, with blunter features,
a broader head; his skin was tougher and thicker, a darker
gray. He was now almost as large as the men, though by no
means so sinewy and quick: when need arose, they moved
with mercurial rapidity.

Once or twice Ern, in a fury, attempted to break the bars
of his booth, only to be prodded with a pole for his trouble,
and he therefore desisted from this unprofitable exercise. He
became fretful and bored. The booths to either side were now
used only for copulation, an activity which Ern observed with
dispassionate interest.

The booth at last was opened. Ern rushed forth, hoping to
surprise his captors and win free, but one man seized him,
another looped a rope around his body. Without ceremony he
was led from the village.

The men offered no hint of their intentions. Jogging along
at a half-trot, they took Ern through the black brush in that
direction known as "sea-left:" which was to say, with the sea
on the left hand. The trail veered inland, rising over bare
hummocks, dropping into dank swales, brimming with rank
black dendrons.

Ahead loomed a great copse of umbrella trees, impressively
tall, each stalk as thick as the body of a man, each billowing
leaf large enough to envelope a half-dozen booths like that in
which Ern had been imprisoned.

Someone had been at work. A number of the trees had
been cut, the poles trimmed and neatly stacked, the leaves cut
into rectangular sheets and draped over ropes. The racks supporting the poles had been built with meticulous accuracy,
and Ern wondered who had done such precise work: certainly not the men of the village, whose construction even
Ern found haphazard.

A path led away through the forest: a path straight as a
string, of constant width, delineated by parallel lines of white
stones: a technical achievement far beyond the capacity of
the men, thought Ern.

The men now became furtive and uneasy. Ern tried to
hang back, certain that whatever the men had in mind was
not to his advantage, but willy-nilly he was jerked forward.

The path made an abrupt turn, marched up a swale between copses of black-brown cycads, turned out upon a field
of soft white moss, at the center of which stood a large and

splendid village. The men, pausing in the shadows, made contemptuous sounds, performed insulting acts—provoked, so Ern suspected, by envy, for the village across the meadow surpassed that of his captors as much as that village excelled the environment of the shallows. There were eight precisely spaced rows of huts, built of sawed planks, decorated or given symbolic import by elaborate designs of blue, maroon and black. At the sea-right and sea-left ends of the central avenue stood larger constructions with high-peaked roofs, shingled, like all the others, with slabs of biotite. Notably absent were disorder and refuse; this village, unlike the village of the single-crested men, was fastidiously neat. Behind the village rose the great bluff Ern had noticed on his exploration of the coast.

At the edge of the meadow stood a row of six stakes, and to the first of these the men tied Ern.

"This is the village of the 'Twos'," declared one of the men. "Folk such as yourself. Do not mention that we cut your scalp or affairs will go badly."

They moved back, taking cover under a bank of worm plants. Ern strained at his bonds, convinced that no matter what the eventuality, it could not be to his benefit.

The villagers had taken note of Ern. Ten persons set forth across the meadow. In front came four splendid "Twos," stepping carefully, with an exaggerated strutting gait, followed by six young One-girls, astoundingly urbane in gowns of wadded umbrella leaf. The girls had been disciplined; they no longer used their ordinary sinuous motion but walked in a studied simulation of the Two attitudes. Ern stared in fascination. The "Twos" appeared to be of his own sort, sturdier and heavier than the cleaver-headed "Ones."

The pair in the van apparently shared equal authority. They comported themselves with canonical dignity, and their garments—fringed shawls of black, brown and purple, boots of gray membrane with metal clips, metal filigree greaves—were formalized and elaborate. He on the stormward side wore a crest of glittering metal barbs; he on the darkward side a double row of tall black plumes. The Twos at their back seemed of somewhat lesser prestige. They wore caps of complicated folds and tucks and carried halberds three times their own length. At the rear walked the One-girls, carrying parcels. Ern saw them to be members of his own class, part of the group which had been led away after the selection ritual. Their skin had been stained dark red and yellow; they wore dull yellow caps, yellow shawls, yellow sandals, and walked with the mincing delicate rigidity in which they had been schooled.

The foremost Twos, halting at either side of Ern, examined him with portentous gravity. The halberdiers fixed him with a minatory stare. The girls posed in self-conscious attitudes. The Twos squinted in puzzlement at the double ridges of scar tissue along his scalp. They arrived at a dubious consensus: "He appears sound, if somewhat gross of body and oddly ridged."

One of the halberdiers, propping his weapon against a stake, unbound Ern, who stood tentatively half of a mind to take to his heels. The Two wearing the crest of metal barbs inquired,

"Do you speak?"

"Yes."

"You must say 'Yes, Preceptor of the Storm Dazzle'; such is the form."

Ern found the admonition puzzling, but no more so than the other attributes of the Twos. His best interests, so he decided lay in cautious cooperation. The Twos, while arbitrary and capricious, apparently did not intend him harm. The girls arranged the parcels beside the stake: payment, so it seemed, to the One-men.

"Come then," commanded he of the black plumes. "Watch your feet, walk correctly! Do not swing your arms; you are a Two, an important individual; you must act appropriately, according to the Way."

"Yes, Preceptor of the Storm Dazzle."

"You will address me as 'Preceptor of the Dark Chill'!"

Confused and apprehensive, Ern was marched across the meadow of pale moss. The trail, demarcated now by lines of black stones, bestrewn with black gravel, and glistening in the damp, exactly bisected the meadow, which was lined to either side by tall black-brown fan-trees. First walked the preceptors, then Ern, then the halberdiers and finally the six One-girls.

The trail connected with the central avenue of the village, which opened at the center into a square plaza paved with squares of wood. To the darkward side of the plaza stood a tall black tower supporting a set of peculiar black objects; on the stormward side an identical white tower presented lightning symbols. Across and set back in a widening of the avenue was a long two-story hall, to which Ern was conducted and lodged in a cubicle.

A third pair of Twos, of rank higher than the halberdiers but lower than the Preceptors—the 'Pedagogue of the Storm Dazzle' and the 'Pedagogue of the Dark Chill'—took Ern in charge. He was washed, anointed with oil, and again the weals along his scalp received a puzzled inspection. Ern began to suspect that the Ones had used duplicity; that, in order to sell him to the Twos, they had simulated double ridges across his scalp; and that, after all, he was merely a peculiar variety of One. It was indeed a fact that his sexual parts resembled those of the One-men rather than the epicene, or perhaps atrophied, organs of the Twos. The suspicion made him more uneasy than ever, and he was relieved when the pedagogues brought him a cap, half of silver scales, half of glossy black bird-fiber, which covered his scalp, and a shawl hanging across his chest and belted at the waist, which concealed his sex organs.

As with every other aspect and activity of the Two-village there were niceties of usage in regard to the cap. "The Way requires that in low-ceremonial activity, you must stand with black toward Night and silver toward Chaos. If a ritual or other urgency impedes, reverse your cap."

This was the simplest and least complicated of the decorums to be observed.

The Pedagogues found much to criticize in Ern's deportment.

"You are somewhat more crude and gross than the usual cadet," remarked the Pedagogue of Storm Dazzle. "The injury to your head has affected your condition."

"You will be carefully schooled," the Pedagogue of Dark Chill told him. "As of this moment, consider yourself a mental void."

A dozen other young Twos, including four from Ern's class, were undergoing tutelage. As instruction was on an individual basis, Ern saw little of them. He studied diligently and assimilated knowledge with a facility which won him grudging compliments. When he seemed proficient in primary methods, he was introduced to cosmology and religion. "We inhabit the Narrow Land," declared the Pedagogue of Storm Dazzle. "It extends forever! How can we assert this with such confidence? Because we know that the opposing principles of Storm and Dark Chill, being divine, are infinite. Therefore, the Narrow Land, the region of confrontation, likewise is infinite."

Ern ventured a question. "What exists behind the wall of storm?"

"There is no 'behind.' STORM-CHAOS *is*, and dazzles the dark with his lightnings. This is the masculine principle. DARK-CHILL, the female principle, *is*. She accepts the rage and fire and quells it. We Twos partake of each, we are at equilibrium, and hence excellent."

Ern broached a perplexing topic: "The Two-women do not produce eggs?"

"There are neither Two-women nor Two-men! We are brought into being by dual-divine intervention, when a pair of eggs in a One-woman's clutch are put down in juxtaposition. Through alternation, these are always male and female and so yield a double individual, neutral and dispassionate, symbolized by the paired cranial ridges. One-men and One-women are incomplete, forever driven by the urge to couple; only fusion yields the true Two."

It was evident to Ern that questioning disturbed the Pedagogues, so he desisted from further interrogation, not wishing to call attention to his unusual attributes. During instruction he had sensibly increased in size. The combs of maturity were growing up over his scalp; his sexual organs had developed noticeably. Both, luckily, were concealed, by cap and shawl. In some fashion he was different from other Twos, and the Pedagogues, should they discover this fact, would feel dismay and confusion, at the very least.

Other matters troubled Ern: namely the impulses aroused within himself by the slave One-girls. Such tendencies were defined to be ignoble! This was no way for a Two to act! The Pedagogues would be horrified to learn of his leanings. But if he were not a Two—what was he?

Ern tried to quell his hot blood by extreme diligence. He began to study the Two technology, which like every other aspect of Two society was rationalized in terms of formal dogma. He learned the methods of collecting bog iron, of smelting, casting, forging, hardening and tempering. Occasionally he wondered how the skills had first been evolved, inasmuch as empiricism, as a mode of thought, was antithetical to the Dual Way.

Ern thoughtlessly touched upon the subject during a recitation. Both Pedagogues were present. The Pedagogue of

Storm-Dazzle replied, somewhat tartly, that all knowledge was a dispensation of the two Basic Principles.

"In any event," stated the Pedagogue of Dark-Chill, "the matter is irrelevant. What is, *is*, and by this token is optimum."

"Indeed," remarked the Pedagogue of Storm-Dazzle, "the very fact that you have formed this inquiry betrays a disorganized mind, more typical of a 'Freak' than a Two."

"What is a 'Freak'?" asked Ern.

The Pedagogue of Dark-Chill made a stern gesture. "Once again your mentality tends to random association and discontent with authority!"

"Respectfully, Pedagogue of Dark-Chill, I wish only to learn the nature of 'wrong,' so that I may know its distinction from 'right.'"

"It suffices that you imbue yourself with 'right,' with no reference whatever to 'wrong'!"

With this viewpoint Ern was forced to be content. The Pedagogues, leaving the chamber, glanced back at him. Ern heard a fragment of their muttered conversation. "—surprising perversity—" "—but for the evidence of the cranial ridges—"

In perturbation Ern walked back and forth across his cubicle. He was different from the other cadets: so much was clear.

At the refectory, where the cadets were brought nutriment by One-girls, Ern covertly scrutinized his fellows. While only little less massive than himself, they seemed differently proportioned, almost cylindrical, with features and protrusions less prominent. If he were different, what kind of person was he? A 'Freak'? What was a 'Freak'? A masculine Two? Ern was inclined to credit this theory, for it explained his interest in the One-girls, and he turned to watch them gliding back and forth with trays. In spite of their One-ness, they were undeniably appealing . . .

Thoughtfully Ern returned to his cubicle. In due course a One-girl came past. Ern summoned her into the cubicle and made his wishes known. She showed surprise and uneasiness, though no great disinclination. "You are supposed to be neutral; what will everyone think?"

"Nothing whatever, if they are unaware of the situation."

"True. But is the matter feasible? I am One and you are a Two—"

"The matter may or may not be feasible; how will the

truth be known unless it is attempted, orthodoxy notwith-
standing?"

"Well, then, as you will . . ."

A monitor looked into the cubicle, to stare dumbfounded.
"What goes on here?" He looked more closely, then tumbled
backward into the compound to shout: "A Freak, a Freak!
Here among us, a Freak! To arms, kill the Freak!"

Ern thrust the girl outside. "Mingle with the others, deny
everything. I now feel that I must leave." He ran out upon
the central avenue, looked up and down. The halberdiers, in-
formed of emergency, were arraying themselves in formally
appropriate gear. Ern took advantage of the delay to run
from the village. In pursuit came the Twos, calling threats
and ritual abuse. The sea-right path toward the pole forest
and the swamp was closed to him; Ern fled sea-left, toward
the great bluff. Dodging among fan trees and banks of
wormweed, finally hiding under a bank of fungus, he gained
a respite while the halberdiers raced past.

Emerging from his covert, Ern stood uncertainly, wondering which way to go. Freak or not, the Twos had exhibited
what seemed an irrational antagonism. Why had they attacked him? He had performed no damage, perpetrated no
wilful deception. The fault lay with the Ones. In order to de-
ceive the Twos they had scarred Ern's head—a situation for
which Ern could hardly be held accountable. Bewildered and
depressed, Ern started toward the shore, where at least he
could find food. Crossing a peat bog he was sighted by the
halberdiers, who instantly set up the outcry: "Freak! Freak!
Freak!" And again Ern was forced to run for his life, up
through a forest of mingled cycads and pole-trees, toward the
great bluff which now loomed ahead.

A massive stone wall barred his way: a construction obviously of great age, overgrown with black and brown lichen.
Ern ran staggering and wobbling along the wall, with the halberdiers close upon him, still screaming: "Freak! Freak!
Freak!"

A gap appeared in the wall. Ern jumped through to the opposite side, ducked behind a clump of feather-bush. The halberdiers stopped short in front of the gap, their cries stilled,
and now they seemed to be engaged in controversy.

Ern waited despondently for discovery and death, since the
bush offered scant concealment. One of the halberdiers at last
ventured gingerly through the wall, only to give a startled
grunt and jump back.

There were receding footsteps, then silence. Ern crawled cautiously from his hiding place, and went to peer through the gap. The Twos had departed. Peculiar, thought Ern. They must have known he was close at hand . . . He turned. Ten paces distant the largest man he had yet seen leaned on a sword, inspecting him with a brooding gaze. The man was almost twice the size of the largest Two. He wore a dull brown smock of soft leather, a pair of shining metal wristbands. His skin was a heavy rugose gray, tough as horn; at the joints of his arms and legs were bony juts, ridges and buttresses, which gave him the semblance of enormous power. His skull was broad, heavy, harshly indented and ridged; his eyes were blazing crystals in deep shrouded sockets. Along his scalp ran three serrated ridges. In addition to his sword, he carried, slung over his shoulder, a peculiar metal device with a long nozzle. He advanced a slow step. Ern swayed back, but for some reason beyond his own knowing was dissuaded from taking to his heels.

The man spoke, in a hoarse voice: "Why do they hunt you?"

Ern took courage from the fact that the man had not killed him out of hand. "They called me 'Freak' and drove me forth."

" 'Freak'?" The Three considered Ern's scalp. "You are a Two."

"The Ones cut my head to make scars, then sold me to the Twos." Ern felt the weals. On either side and at the center, almost as prominent as the scars, were the crests of an adult, three in number. They were growing apace; even had he not compromised himself, the Twos must have found him out on the first occasion he removed his cap. He said humbly: "It appears that I am a 'Freak' like yourself."

The Three made a brusque sound. "Come with me."

They walked back through the grove, to a path which slanted up the bluff, then swung to the side and entered a valley. Beside a pond rose a great stone hall flanked by two towers with steep conical roofs—in spite of age and dilapidation a structure to stagger Ern's imagination.

By a timber portal they entered a courtyard which seemed to Ern a place of unparalleled charm. At the far end boulders and a great overhanging slab created the effect of a grotto. Within were trickling water, growths of feathery black moss, pale cycads, a settle padded with woven reed and sphagnum. The open area was a swamp-garden, exhaling the odors of reed, water-soaked vegetation, resinous wood. Remarkable, thought Ern, as well as enchanting: neither the Ones nor the Twos contrived except for an immediate purpose.

The Three took Ern across the court into a stone chamber, also half-open to the refreshing drizzle, carpeted with packed sphagnum. Under the shelter of the ceiling were the appurtenances of the Three's existence: crocks and bins, a table, a cabinet, tools and implements.

The Three pointed to a bench. "Sit."

Ern gingerly obeyed.

"You are hungry?"

"No."

"How was your imposture discovered?"

Ern related the circumstances which led to his exposure. The Three showed no disapproval, which gave Ern encouragement. "I had long suspected that I was something other than a 'Two'."

"You are obviously a 'Three'," said his host. "Unlike the neuter Twos, Threes are notably masculine, which explains your inclinations for the One-woman. Unluckily there are no Three females." He looked at Ern. "They did not tell how you were born?"

"I am the fusion of One-eggs."

"True. The One-woman lays eggs of alternate sex, in clutches of three. The pattern is male-female-male; such is the nature of her organism. A sheath forms on the interior of her ovipositor; as the eggs emerge, a sphincter closes, to encapsulate the eggs. If she is careless, she will fail to separate the eggs and will put down a clutch with two eggs in contact. The male breaks into the female shell; there is fusion; a Two is hatched. At the rarest of intervals three eggs are so joined. One male fuses with the female, then, so augmented, he breaks into the final egg and assimilates the other male. The result is a male Three."

Ern recalled his first memory. "I was alone. I broke into the male-female shell. We fought at length."

The Three reflected for a lengthy period. Ern wondered if he had committed an annoyance. Finally the Three said, "I am named Mazar the Final. Now that you are here I can be known as 'the Final' no longer. I am accustomed to solitude; I have become old and severe; you may find me poor company. If such is the case, you are free to pursue existence elsewhere. If you choose to stay, I will teach you what I know, which is perhaps pointless activity, since the Twos will presently come in a great army to kill us both."

"I will stay," said Ern. "As of now I know only the ceremonies of the Twos, which I may never put to use. Are there no other Threes?"

"The Twos have killed all—all but Mazar the Final."

"And Ern."

"And now Ern."

"What of sea-left and sea-right, beyond the rivers, along other shores? Are there no more men?"

"Who knows? The Wall of Storm confronts the Wall of Dark; the Narrow Land extends—how far? Who knows? If to infinity then all possibilities must be realized; then there are other Ones, Twos and Threes. If the Narrow Land terminates at Chaos, then we may be alone."

"I have traveled sea-right and sea-left until wide rivers stopped me," said Ern. "The Narrow Land continued without any sign of coming to an end. I believe that it must extend to infinity; in fact, it is hard to conceive of a different situation."

"Perhaps, perhaps," said Mazar gruffly. "Come." He conducted Ern about the hall, through workshops and repositories, chambers crowded with mementoes, trophies and nameless paraphernalia.

"Who used these marvelous objects? Were there many Threes?"

"At one time there were many," intoned Mazar, in a voice as hoarse and dreary as the sound of wind. "It was so long ago that I cannot put words to the thought. I am the last."

"Why were there so many then and so few now?"

"It is a melancholy tale. A One-tribe lived along the shore, with customs different from the Ones of the swamp. They were a gentle people, and they were ruled by a Three who had been born by accident. He was Mena the Origin, and he caused the women to produce clutches with the eggs purposely joined, so that a large number of Threes came into being. It was a great era. We were dissatisfied with the harsh life of the Ones, the rigid life of the Twos; we created a new existence. We learned the use of iron and steel, we built this hall and many more; the Ones and Twos both learned from us and profited."

"Why did they war upon you?"

"By our freedom we incurred their fear. We set out to explore the Narrow Land. We traveled many leagues sea-left and sea-right. An expedition penetrated the Dark-Chill to a wilderness of ice, so dark that the explorers walked with torches. We built a raft and sent it to drift under the Wall of Storm. There were three Ones aboard. The raft was tethered with a long cable; when we pulled it back the Ones had been riven by dazzle and were dead. By these acts we infuriated the Two preceptors. They declared us impious and marshaled the Ones of the swamp. They massacred the Ones of the shore, then they made war on the Threes. Ambush, poison, pitfall: they showed no mercy. We killed Twos; there were always more Twos, but never more Threes.

"I could tell long tales of the war, how each of my comrades met death. Of them all, I am the last. I never go beyond the wall and the Twos are not anxious to attack me, for they fear my fire gun. But enough for now. Go where you will, except beyond the wall, where the Twos are dangerous. There is food in the bins; you may rest in the moss. Reflect upon what you see; and when you have questions, I will answer."

Mazar went his way. Ern refreshed himself in the falling water of the grotto, ate from the bins, then walked upon the gray meadow to consider what he had learned. Here Mazar, becoming curious, discovered him. "Well then," asked Mazar, "and what do you think now?"

"I understand many things which have puzzled me," said Ern. "Also I regret leaving the One-girl, who showed a cooperative disposition."

"This varies according to the individual," said Mazar. "In the olden times we employed many such as domestics, though their mental capacity is not great."

"If there were Three-women, would they not produce eggs and eventually Three-children?"

Mazar made a brusque gesture. "There are no Three-women; there have never been Three-women. The process allows none to form."

"What if the process were controlled?"

"Bah. The ovulation of One-women is not susceptible to our control."

"Long ago," said Ern, "I watched a One-woman preparing her nest. She laid in clutches of three. If sufficient eggs were collected, rearranged and joined, in some cases the female principle would dominate."

"This is an unorthodox proposal," said Mazar, "and to my knowledge has never been tried. It cannot be feasible . . ."

Such women might not be fertile. Or they might be freaks indeed."

"We are a product of the process," Ern argued. "Because there are two male eggs to the clutch, we are masculine. If there were two female and one male, or three female, why should not the result be female? As for fertility, we have no knowledge until the matter is put to test."

"The process is unthinkable!" roared Mazar, drawing himself erect, crests extended. "I will hear no more!"

Dazed by the fury of the old Three's response, Ern stood limp. Slowly he turned and started to walk sea-right, toward the wall.

"Where are you going?" Mazar called after him.

"To the swamps."

"And what will you do there?"

"I will find eggs and try to help a Three-woman into being."

Mazar glared and Ern prepared to flee for his life. Then Mazar said, "If your scheme is sound, all my comrades are dead in vain. Existence becomes a mockery."

"Perhaps nothing will come of the notion," said Ern. "If so, nothing is different."

"The venture is dangerous," grumbled Mazar. "The Twos will be alert."

"I will go down to the shore and swim to the swamp; they will never notice me. In any case, I have no better use to which to put my life."

"Go then," said Mazar in his hoarsest voice. "I am old and without enterprise. Perhaps our race may yet be regenerated. Go then, take care and return safely. You and I are the only Threes alive."


Mazar patrolled the wall. At times he ventured out into the pole-forest, listening, peering down toward the Two village. Ern had been gone a long time, or so it seemed. At last: far-off alarms, the cry of "Freak! Freak! Freak!"

Recklessly, three crests furiously erect, Mazar plunged toward the sound. Ern appeared through the trees, haggard, streaked with mud, carrying a rush-basket. In frantic pursuit came Two halberdiers and somewhat to the side a band of painted One-men. "This way!" roared Mazar. "To the wall!" He brought forth his fire-gun. The halberdiers, in a frenzy, ignored the threat. Ern tottered past him; Mazar pointed the projector, pulled the trigger: flame enveloped four of the halberdiers who ran thrashing and flailing through the forest. The others halted. Mazar and Ern retreated to the wall, passed through the gap. The halberdiers, excited to rashness, leapt after them. Mazar swung his sword; one of the Twos lost his head. The others retreated in panic, keening in horror at so much death.

Ern slumped upon the ground, cradling the eggs upon his body.

"How many?" demanded Mazar.

"I found two nests. I took three clutches from each."

"Each nest is separate and each clutch as well? Eggs from different nests may not fuse."

"Each is separate."

Mazar carried the corpse to the gap in the wall, flung it forth, then threw the head at the skulking One-men. None came to challenge him.

Once more in the hall Mazar arranged the eggs on a stone settle. He made a sound of satisfaction. "In each clutch are two round eggs and one oval: male and female; and we need not guess at the combinations." He reflected a moment. "Two males and a female produce the masculine Three; two females and a male should exert an equal influence in the opposite direction . . . There will necessarily be an excess of male eggs. They will yield two masculine Threes; possibly more, if three male eggs are able to fuse." He made a thoughtful sound. "It is a temptation to attempt the fusion of four eggs."

"In this case I would urge caution," suggested Ern.

Mazar drew back in surprise and displeasure. "Is your wisdom so much more profound than mine?"

Ern made a polite gesture of self-effacement, one of the graces learned at the Two school. "I was born on the shallows, among the water-babies. Our great enemy was the ogre who lived in a slough. While I searched for eggs, I saw him again. He is larger than you and I together; his limbs are gross; his head is malformed and hung over with red wattles. Upon his head stand four crests."

Mazar was silent. He said at last: "We are Threes. Best that we produce other Threes. Well then, to work."

The eggs lay in the cool mud, three paces from the water of the pond.

"Now to wait," said Mazar. "To wait and wonder."

"I will help them survive," said Ern. "I will bring them food and keep them safe. And—if they are female . . ."

"There will be two females," declared Mazar. "Of this I am certain. I am old—but, well, we shall see."

# The Masquerade on Dicantropus

Two puzzles dominated the life of Jim Root. The first, the pyramid out in the desert, tickled and prodded his curiosity, while the second, the problem of getting along with his wife, kept him keyed to a high pitch of anxiety and apprehension. At the moment the problem had crowded the mystery of the pyramid into a lost alley of his brain.

Eyeing his wife uneasily, Root decided that she was in for another of her fits. The symptoms were familiar—a jerking over of the pages of an old magazine, her tense back and bolt-upright posture, her pointed silence, the compression at the corners of her mouth.

With no preliminary motion she threw the magazine across the room, jumped to her feet. She walked to the doorway, stood looking out across the plain, fingers tapping on the sill. Root heard her voice, low, as if not meant for him to hear.

"Another day of this and I'll lose what little's left of my mind."

Root approached warily. If he could be compared to a Labrador retriever, then his wife was a black panther—a woman tall and well-covered with sumptuous flesh. She had black flowing hair and black flashing eyes. She lacquered her fingernails and wore black lounge pajamas even on desiccated deserted inhospitable Dicantropus.

"Now, dear," said Root, "take it easy. Certainly it's not as bad as all that."

She whirled and Root was surprised by the intensity in her eyes. "It's not bad, you say? Very well for you to talk—*you* don't care for anything human to begin with. I'm sick of it. Do you hear? I want to go back to Earth! I never want to see another planet in my whole life. I never want to hear the word archaeology, I never want to see a rock or a bone or a microscope—"

31

She flung a wild gesture around the room that included a number of rocks, bones, microscopes, as well as books, specimens in bottles, photographic equipment, a number of native artifacts.

Root tried to soothe her with logic. "Very few people are privileged to live on an outside planet, dear."

"They're in their right minds. If I'd known what it was like, I'd never have come out here." Her voice dropped once more. "Same old dirt every day, same stinking natives, same vile canned food, nobody to talk to—"

Root uncertainly picked up and laid down his pipe. "Lie down, dear," he said with unconvincing confidence. "Take a nap! Things will look different when you wake up."

Stabbing him with a look, she turned and strode out into the blue-white glare of the sun. Root followed more slowly, bringing Barbara's sun-helmet and adjusting his own. Automatically he cocked an eye up the antenna, the reason for the station and his own presence, Dicantropus being a relay point for ULR messages between Clave II and Polaris. The antenna stood as usual, polished metal tubing four hundred feet high.

Barbara halted by the shore of the lake, a brackish pond in the neck of an old volcano, one of the few natural bodies of water on the planet. Root silently joined her, handed her her sun-helmet. She jammed it on her head, walked away.

Root shrugged, watched her as she circled the pond to a clump of feather-fronded cycads. She flung herself down, relaxed into a sulky lassitude, her back to a big gray-green trunk, and seemed intent on the antics of the natives—owlish leather-gray little creatures popping back and forth into holes in their mound.

This was a hillock a quarter-mile long, covered with spine-scrub and a rusty black creeper. With one exception it was the only eminence as far as the eye could reach, horizon to horizon, across the baked helpless expanse of the desert.

The exception was the stepped pyramid, the mystery of which irked Root. It was built of massive granite blocks, set without mortar but cut so carefully that hardly a crack could be seen. Early on his arrival Root had climbed all over the pyramid, unsuccessfully seeking entrance.

When finally he brought out his atomite torch to melt a hole in the granite a sudden swarm of natives pushed him back and in the pidgin of Dicantropus gave him to understand that entrance was forbidden. Root desisted with reluctance, and had been consumed by curiosity ever since . . .

Who had built the pyramid? In style it resembled the *ziggurats* of ancient Assyria. The granite had been set with a skill unknown, so far as Root could see, to the natives. But if not the natives—who? A thousand times Root had chased the question through his brain. Were the natives debased relics of a once-civilized race? If so, why were there no other ruins? And what was the purpose of the pyramid? A temple? A mausoleum? A treasure-house? Perhaps it was entered from below by a tunnel.

As Root stood on the shore of the lake, looking across the desert, the questions flicked automatically through his mind though without their usual pungency. At the moment the problem of soothing his wife lay heavy on his mind. He debated a few moments whether or not to join her; perhaps she had cooled off and might like some company. He circled the pond and stood looking down at her glossy black hair.

"I came over here to be alone," she said without accent and the indifference chilled him more than an insult.

"I thought—that maybe you might like to talk," said Root. "I'm very sorry, Barbara, that you're unhappy."

Still she said nothing, sitting with her head pressed back against the treetrunk.

"We'll go home on the next supply ship," Root said. "Let's see, there should be one—"

"Three months and three days," said Barbara flatly.

Root shifted his weight, watched her from the corner of his eye. This was a new manifestation. Tears, recriminations, anger—there had been plenty of these before.

"We'll try to keep amused till then," he said desperately. "Let's think up some games to play. Maybe badminton—or we could do more swimming."

Barbara snorted in sharp sarcastic laughter. "With things like that popping up around you?" She gestured to one of the Dicantrops who had lazily paddled close. She narrowed her eyes, leaned forward. "What's that he's got around his neck?"

Root peered. "Looks like a diamond necklace more than anything else."

"My Lord!" whispered Barbara.

Root walked down to the water's edge. "Hey, boy!" The Dicantrop turned his great velvety eyes in their sockets. "Come here!"

Barbara joined him as the native paddled close.

"Let's see what you've got there," said Root, leaning close to the necklace.

"Why, those are *beautiful!*" breathed his wife.

Root chewed his lip thoughtfully. "They certainly look like diamonds. The setting might be platinum or iridium. Hey, boy, where did you get these?"

The Dicantrop paddled backward. "We find."

"Where?"

The Dicantrop blew froth from his breath-holes but it seemed to Root as if his eyes had glanced momentarily toward the pyramid.

"You find in big pile of rock?"

"No," said the native and sank below the surface.

Barbara returned to her seat by the tree, frowned at the water. Root joined her. For a moment there was silence. Then Barbara said, "That pyramid must be full of things like that!"

Root made a deprecatory noise in his throat. "Oh—I suppose it's possible."

"Why don't you go out and see?"

"I'd like to—but you know it would make trouble."

"You could go out at night."

"No," said Root uncomfortably. "It's really not right. If they want to keep the thing closed up and secret it's their business. After all it belongs to them."

"How do you know it does?" his wife insisted, with a hard and sharp directness. "They didn't build it and probably never put those diamonds there." Scorn crept into her voice. "Are you afraid?"

"Yes," said Root. "I'm afraid. There's an awful lot of them and only two of us. That's one objection. But the other, most important—"

Barbara let herself slump back against the trunk. "I don't want to hear it."

Root, now angry himself, said nothing for a minute. Then, thinking of the three months and three days till the arrival of the supply ship, he said, "It's no use our being disagreeable. It just makes it harder on both of us. I made a mistake bringing you out here and I'm sorry. I thought you'd enjoy the experience, just the two of us alone on a strange planet—"

Barbara was not listening to him. Her mind was elsewhere.

*"Barbara!"*

*"Shh!"* she snapped. "Be still! Listen!"

He jerked his head up. The air vibrated with a far *thrum-m-m-m*. Root sprang out into the sunlight, scanned the sky. The sound grew louder. There was no question about it, a ship was dropping down from space.

Root ran into the station, flipped open the communicator—but there were no signals coming in. He returned to the door and watched as the ship sank down to a bumpy rough landing two hundred yards from the station.

It was a small ship, the type rich men sometimes used as private yachts, but old and battered. It sat in a quiver of hot air, its tubes creaking and hissing as they cooled. Root approached.

The dogs on the port began to turn, the port swung open. A man stood in the opening. For a moment he teetered on loose legs, then fell headlong.

Root, springing forward, caught him before he struck ground. "Barbara!" Root called. His wife approached. "Take his feet. We'll carry him inside. He's sick."

They laid him on the couch and his eyes opened halfway.

"What's the trouble?" asked Root. "Where do you feel sick?"

"My legs are like ice," husked the man. "My shoulders ache. I can't breathe."

"Wait till I look in the book," muttered Root. He pulled out the Official Spaceman's Self-help Guide, traced down the symptoms. He looked across to the sick man. "You been anywhere near Alphard?"

"Just came from there," panted the man.

"Looks like you got a dose of Lyma's Virus. A shot of mycosetin should fix you up, according to the book."

He inserted an ampule into the hypo-spray, pressed the tip to his patient's arm, pushed the plunger home. "That should do it—according to the *Guide*."

"Thanks," said his patient. "I feel better already." He closed his eyes. Root stood up, glanced at Barbara. She was scrutinizing the man with a peculiar calculation. Root looked down again, seeing the man for the first time. He was young, perhaps thirty, thin but strong with a tight nervous muscularity. His face was lean, almost gaunt, his skin very bronzed. He had short black hair, heavy black eyebrows, a long jaw, a thin high nose.

Root turned away. Glancing at his wife he foresaw the future with a sick certainty.

He washed out the hypospray, returned the Guide to the rack, all with a sudden self-conscious awkwardness. When he turned around, Barbara was staring at him with wide thoughtful eyes. Root slowly left the room.

A day later Marville Landry was on his feet and when he had shaved and changed his clothes there was no sign of the illness. He was by profession a mining engineer, so he revealed to Root, en route to a contract on Thuban XIV.

The virus had struck swiftly and only by luck had he noticed the proximity of Dicantropus on his charts. Rapidly weakening, he had been forced to decelerate so swiftly and land so uncertainly that he feared his fuel was low. And indeed, when they went out to check, they found only enough fuel to throw the ship a hundred feet into the air.

Landry shook his head ruefully. "And there's a ten-million-munit contract waiting for me on Thuban Fourteen."

Said Root dismally, "The supply packets' due in three months."

Landry winced. "Three months—in this hell-hole? That's murder." They returned to the station. "How do you stand it here?"

Barbara heard him. "We don't. I've been on the verge of hysterics every minute the last six months. Jim"—she made a wry grimace toward her husband—"he's got his bones and rocks and the antenna. He's not too much company."

"Maybe I can help out," Landry offered airily.

"Maybe," she said with a cool blank glance at Root. Presently she left the room, walking more gracefully now, with an air of mysterious gaiety.

Dinner that evening was a gala event. As soon as the sun took its blue glare past the horizon Barbara and Landry carried a table down to the lake and there they set it with all the splendor the station could afford. With no word to Root she pulled the cork on the gallon of brandy he had been nursing for a year and served generous highballs with canned lime-juice, Maraschino cherries and ice.

For a space, with the candles glowing and evoking lambent ghosts in the highballs, even Root was gay. The air was wonderfully cool and the sands of the desert spread white and clean as damask out into the dimness. So they feasted on canned fowl and mushrooms and frozen fruit and drank deep of Root's brandy, and across the pond the natives watched from the dark.

And presently, while Root grew sleepy and dull, Landry became gay, and Barbara sparkled—the complete hostess, charming, witty and the Dicantropus night tinkled and throbbed with her laughter. She and Landry toasted each other and exchanged laughing comments at Root's expense—who now sat slumping, stupid, half-asleep. Finally he lurched to his feet and stumbled off to the station.

On the table by the lake the candles burnt low. Barbara poured more brandy. Their voices became murmurs and at last the candles guttered.

In spite of any human will to hold time in blessed darkness, morning came and brought a day of silence and averted eyes. Then other days and nights succeeded each other and time proceeded as usual. And there was now little pretense at the station.

Barbara frankly avoided Root and when she had occasion to speak her voice was one of covert amusement. Landry, secure, confident, aquiline, had a trick of sitting back and looking from one to the other as if inwardly chuckling over the whole episode. Root preserved a studied calm and spoke in a subdued tone which conveyed no meaning other than the sense of his words.

There were a few minor clashes. Entering the bathroom one morning Root found Landry shaving with his razor. Without heat Root took the shaver out of Landry's hand.

For an instant Landry stared blankly, then wrenched his mouth into the beginnings of a snarl.

Root smiled almost sadly. "Don't get me wrong, Landry. There's a difference between a razor and a woman. The razor is mine. A human being can't be owned. Leave my personal property alone."

Landry's eyebrows rose. "Man, you're crazy." He turned away. "Heat's got you."

The days went past and now they were unchanging as before but unchanging with a new leaden tension. Words became even fewer and dislike hung like tattered tinsel. Every motion, every line of the body, became a detestable sight, an evil which the other flaunted deliberately.

Root burrowed almost desperately into his rocks and bones, peered through his microscope, made a thousand

measurements, a thousand notes. Landry and Barbara fell
into the habit of taking long walks in the evening, usually out
to the pyramid, then slowly back across the quiet cool sand.

The mystery of the pyramid suddenly fascinated Landry
and he even questioned Root.

"I've no idea," said Root. "Your guess is as good as mine.
All I know is that the natives don't want anyone trying to get
into it."

"Mph," said Landry, gazing across the desert. "No telling
what's inside. Barbara said one of the natives was wearing a
diamond necklace worth thousands."

"I suppose anything's possible," said Root. He had noticed
the acquisitive twitch to Landry's mouth, the hook of the fingers. "You'd better not get any ideas. I don't want any trouble with the natives. Remember that, Landry."

Landry asked with seeming mildness, "Do you have any
authority over that pyramid?"

"No," said Root shortly. "None whatever."

"It's not—yours?" Landry sardonically accented the word
and Root remembered the incident of the shaver.

"No."

"Then," said Landry, rising, "mind your own business."

He left the room.

During the day Root noticed Landry and Barbara deep in
conversation and he saw Landry rummaging through his ship.
At dinner no single word was spoken.

As usual, when the afterglow had died to a cool blue glimmer, Barbara and Landry strolled off into the desert. But
tonight Root watched after them and he noticed a pack on
Landry's shoulders and Barbara seemed to be carrying a
handbag.

He paced back and forth, puffing furiously at his pipe.
Landry was right—it was none of his business. If there were
profit, he wanted none of it. And if there were danger, it
would strike only those who provoked it. Or would it? Would
he, Root, be automatically involved because of his association
with Landry and Barbara? To the Dicantrops, a man was a
man, and if one man needed punishment, all men did likewise.

Would there be—killing? Root puffed at his pipe, chewed
the stem, blew smoke out in gusts between his teeth. In a
way he was responsible for Barbara's safety. He had taken

her from a sheltered life on Earth. He shook his head, put down his pipe, went to the drawer where he kept his gun. It was gone.

Root looked vacantly across the room. Landry had it. No telling how long since he'd taken it. Root went to the kitchen, found a meat-axe, tucked it inside his jumper, set out across the desert.

He made a wide circle in order to approach the pyramid from behind. The air was quiet and dark and cool as water in an old well. The crisp sand sounded faintly under his feet. Above him spread the sky and the sprinkle of the thousand stars. Somewhere up there was the Sun and old Earth.

The pyramid loomed suddenly large and now he saw a glow, heard the muffled clinking of tools. He approached quietly, halted several hundred feet out in the darkness, stood watching, alert to all sounds.

Landry's atomite torch ate at the granite. As he cut, Barbara hooked the detached chunks out into the sand. From time to time Landry stood back, sweating and gasping from radiated heat.

A foot he cut into the granite, two feet, three feet, and Root heard the excited murmur of voices. They were through, into empty space. Careless of watching behind them they sidled through the hole they had cut. Root, more wary, listened, strove to pierce the darkness . . . Nothing.

He sprang forward, hastened to the hole, peered within. The yellow gleam of Landry's torch swept past his eyes. He crept into the hole, pushed his head out into emptiness. The air was cold, smelled of dust and damp rock.

Landry and Barbara stood fifty feet away. In the desultory flash of the lamp Root saw stone walls and a stone floor. The pyramid appeared to be an empty shell. Why then were the natives so particular? He heard Landry's voice, edged with bitterness.

"Not a damn thing, not even a mummy for your husband to gloat over."

Root could sense Barbara shuddering. "Let's go. It gives me the shivers. It's like a dungeon."

"Just a minute, we might as well make sure . . . Hm." He was playing the light on the walls. "That's peculiar."

"What's peculiar?"

"It looks like the stone was sliced with a torch. Notice how it's fused here on the inside . . ."

Root squinted, trying to see. "Strange," he heard Landry mutter. "Outside it's chipped, inside it's cut by a torch. It doesn't look so very old here inside, either."

"The air would preserve it," suggested Barbara dubiously.

"I suppose so—still, old places look old. There's dust and a kind of dullness. This looks raw."

"I don't understand how that could be."

"I don't either. There's something funny somewhere."

Root stiffened. Sound from without? Shuffle of splay feet in the sand—he started to back out. Something pushed him, he sprawled forward, fell. The bright eye of Landry's torch stared in his direction. "What's that?" came a hard voice. "Who's there?"

Root looked over his shoulder. The light passed over him, struck a dozen gray bony forms. They stood quietly just inside the hole, their eyes like balls of black plush.

Root gained his feet. "Hah!" cried Landry. "So *you're* here too."

"Not because I want to be," returned Root grimly.

Landry edged slowly forward, keeping his light on the Dicantrops. He asked Root sharply, "Are these lads dangerous?"

Root appraised the natives. "I don't know."

"Stay still," said one of these in the front rank. "Stay still." His voice was a deep croak.

"Stay still, *hell!*" exclaimed Landry. "We're leaving. There's nothing here I want. Get out of the way." He stepped forward.

"Stay still . . . We kill . . ."

Landry paused.

"What's the trouble now?" interposed Root anxiously. "Surely there's no harm in looking. There's nothing here."

"That is why we kill. Nothing here, now you know. Now you look other place. When you think this place important, then you not look other place. We kill, new man come, he think this place important."

Landry muttered. "Do you get what he's driving at?"

Root said slowly, "I don't know for sure." He addressed the Dicantrop. "We don't care about your secrets. You've no reason to hide things from us."

The native jerked his head. "Then why do you come here? You look for secrets."

Barbara's voice came from behind. "What *is* your secret? Diamonds?"

The native jerked his head again. Amusement? Anger? His emotions, unearthly, could be matched by no earthly words. "Diamonds are nothing—rocks."

"I'd like a carload," Landry muttered under his breath.

"Now look here," said Root persuasively. "You let us out and we won't pry into any of your secrets. It was wrong of us to break in and I'm sorry it happened. We'll repair the damage—"

The Dicantrop made a faint sputtering sound. "You do not understand. You tell other men—pyramid is nothing. Then other men look all around for other thing. They bother, look, look, look. All this no good. You die, everything go like before."

"There's too much talk," said Landry viciously, "and I don't like the sound of it. Let's get out of here." He pulled out Root's gun. "Come on," he snapped at Root, "let's move."

To the natives, "Get out of the way or I'll do some killing myself!"

A rustle of movement from the natives, a thin excited whimper.

"We've got to rush 'em," shouted Landry. "If they get outside they can knock us over as we leave. Let's *go!*"

He sprang forward and Root was close behind. Landry used the gun as a club and Root used his fists and the Dicantrops rattled like cornstalks against the walls. Landry erupted through the hole. Root pushed Barbara through and, kicking back at the natives behind him, struggled out into the air.

Landry's momentum had carried him away from the pyramid, out into a seething mob of Dicantrops. Root, following more slowly, pressed his back to the granite. He sensed the convulsive movement in the wide darkness. "The whole colony must be down here," he shouted into Barbara's ear. For a minute he was occupied with the swarming natives, keeping Barbara behind him as much as possible. The first ledge of granite was about shoulder height.

"Step on my hands," he panted. "I'll shove you up."

"But—Landry!" came Barbara's choked wail.

"Look at that crowd!" bit Root furiously. "We can't do anything." A sudden rush of small bony forms almost overwhelmed him. "Hurry up!"

Whimpering she stepped into his clasped hands. He thrust her up on the first ledge. Shaking off the clawing natives who had leapt on him, he jumped, scrambled up beside her. "Now run!" he shouted in her ear and she fled down the ledge.

From the darkness came a violent cry. "Root! *Root!* For *God's* sake—they've got me down—" Another hoarse yell, rising to a scream of agony. Then silence.

"Hurry!" said Root. They came to the far corner of the pyramid. "Jump down," panted Root. "Down to the ground."

"Landry!" moaned Barbara, teetering at the edge.

"Get *down!*" snarled Root. He thrust her down to the white sand and, seizing her hand, ran across the desert, back toward the station. A minute or so later, with pursuit left behind, he slowed to a trot.

"We should go back," cried Barbara. "Are you going to leave him to those devils?"

Root was silent a moment. Then, choosing his words, he said, "I told him to stay away from the place. Anything that happens to him is his own fault. And whatever it is, it's already happened. There's nothing we can do now."

A dark hulk shouldered against the sky—Landry's ship.

"Let's get in here," said Root. "We'll be safer than in the station."

He helped her into the ship, clamped tight the port. *"Phew!"* He shook his head. "Never thought it would come to this."

He climbed into the pilot's seat, looked out across the desert. Barbara huddled somewhere behind him, sobbing softly.

An hour passed, during which they said no word. Then, without warning, a fiery orange ball rose from the hill across the pond, drifted toward the station. Root blinked, jerked upright in his seat. He scrambled for the ship's machine-gun, yanked at the trigger—without result.

When at last he found and threw off the safety the orange ball hung over the station and Root held his fire. The ball brushed against the antenna—a tremendous explosion spattered to every corner of vision. It seared Root's eyes, threw him to the deck, rocked the ship, left him dazed and half-conscious.

Barbara lay moaning. Root hauled himself to his feet. A seared pit, a tangle of metal, showed where the station had stood. Root dazedly slumped into the seat, started the fuel pump, plunged home the catalyzers. The boat quivered, bumped a few feet along the ground. The tubes sputtered, wheezed.

Root looked at the fuel gauge, looked again. The needle pointed to zero, a fact which Root had known but forgotten. He cursed his own stupidity. Their presence in the ship might have gone ignored if he had not called attention to it.

Up from the hill floated another orange ball. Root jumped for the machine gun, sent out a burst of explosive pellets. Again the roar and the blast and the whole top of the hill was blown off, revealing what appeared to be a smooth strata of black rock.

Root looked over his shoulder to Barbara. "This is it."

"Wha—what do you mean?"

"We can't get away. Sooner or later—" His voice trailed off. He reached up, twisted a dial labelled EMERGENCY. The ship's ULR unit hummed. Root said into the mesh, "Dicantropus station—we're being attacked by natives. Send help at once."

Root sank back into the seat. A tape would repeat his message endlessly until cut off.

Barbara staggered to the seat beside Root. "What were those orange balls?"

"That's what *I've* been wondering—some sort of bomb."

But there were no more of them. And presently the horizon began to glare, the hill became a silhouette on the electric sky. And over their heads the transmitter pulsed an endless message into space.

"How long before we get help?" whispered Barbara.

"Too long," said Root, staring off toward the hill. "They must be afraid of the machine gun—I can't understand what else they're waiting for. Maybe good light."

"They can—" Her voice stopped. She stared. Root stared, held by unbelief—amazement. The hill across the pond was breaking open, crumbling . . .

Root sat drinking brandy with the captain of the supply ship *Method*, which had come to their assistance, and the captain was shaking his head.

"I've seen lots of strange things around this cluster but this masquerade beats everything."

Root said, "It's strange in one way, in another it's as cold and straightforward as ABC. They played it as well as they could and it was pretty darned good. If it hadn't been for that scoundrel Landry they'd have fooled us forever."

The captain banged his glass on the desk, stared at Root. "But *why?*"

Root said slowly, "They liked Dicantropus. It's a hell-hole, a desert to us, but it was heaven to them. They liked the heat, the dryness. But they didn't want a lot of off-world creatures prying into their business—as we surely would have if we'd seen through the masquerade. It must have been an awful shock when the first Earth ship set down here."

"And that pyramid . . ."

"Now that's a strange thing. They were good psychologists, these Dicantrops, as good as you could expect an off-world race to be. If you'll read a report of the first landing, you'll find no mention of the pyramid. Why? Because it wasn't here. Landry thought it looked new. He was right. It *was* new. It was a fraud, a decoy—just strange enough to distract our attention.

"As long as that pyramid sat out there, with me focusing all my mental energy on it, they were safe—and how they must have laughed.. As soon as Landry broke in and discovered the fraud, then it was all over . . .

"That might have been their miscalculation," mused Root. "Assume that they knew nothing of crime, of anti-social action. If everybody did what he was told to do their privacy was safe forever." Root laughed. "Maybe they didn't know human beings so well after all."

The captain refilled the glasses and they drank in silence. "Wonder where they came from," he said at last.

Root shrugged. "I suppose we'll never know. Some other hot dry planet, that's sure. Maybe they were refugees or some peculiar religious sect or maybe they were a colony."

"Hard to say," agreed the captain sagely. "Different race, different psychology. That's what we run into all the time."

"Thank God they weren't vindictive," said Root, half to himself. "No doubt they could have killed us any one of a dozen ways after I'd sent out that emergency call and they had to leave."

"It all ties in," admitted the captain.

Root sipped the brandy, nodded. "Once that ULR signal went out, their isolation was done for. No matter whether we were dead or not, there'd be Earthmen swarming around the station, pushing into their tunnels—and right there went their secret."

And he and the captain silently inspected the hole across

the pond where the tremendous space-ship had lain buried under the spine-scrub and rusty black creeper.

"And once that space-ship was laid bare," Root continued, "there'd be a hullabaloo from here to Fomalhaut. A tremendous mass like that? We'd have to know everything—their space-drive, their history, everything about them. If what they wanted was privacy that would be a thing of the past. If they were a colony from another star they had to protect their secrets the same way we protect ours."

Barbara was standing by the ruins of the station, poking at the tangle with a stick. She turned and Root saw that she held his pipe. It was charred and battered but still recognizable.

She slowly handed it to him.

"Well?" said Root.

She answered in a quiet withdrawn voice: "Now that I'm leaving I think I'll miss Dicantropus." She turned to him, "Jim . . ."

"What?"

"I'd stay on another year if you'd like."

"No," said Root. "I don't like it here myself."

She said, still in the low tone: "Then—you don't forgive me for being foolish . . ."

Root raised his eyebrows. "Certainly I do. I never blamed you in the first place. You're human. Indisputably human."

"Then—why are you acting—like Moses?"

Root shrugged.

"Whether you believe me or not," she said with an averted gaze, "I never—"

He interrupted with a gesture. "What does it matter? Suppose you did—you had plenty of reason to. I wouldn't hold it against you."

"You would—in your heart."

Root said nothing.

"I wanted to hurt you. I was slowly going crazy—and you didn't seem to care one way or another. Told—him I wasn't—your property."

Root smiled his sad smile, "I'm human too."

He made a casual gesture toward the hole where the Dicantrop spaceship had lain. "If you still want diamonds go down that hole with a bucket. There're diamonds big as grapefruit. It's an old volcanic neck, it's the grand-daddy of all diamond mines. I've got a claim staked out around it;

we'll be using diamonds for billiard balls as soon as we get some machinery out here."

They turned slowly back to the *Method*.

"Three's quite a crowd on Dicantropus," said Root thoughtfully. "On Earth, where there're three billion, we can have a little privacy."

# Where Hesperut Falls

My servants will not allow me to kill myself. I have sought self-extinction by every method, from throat-cutting to the intricate routines of Yoga, but so far they have thwarted my most ingenious efforts.

I grow ever more annoyed. What is more personal, more truly one's own, than a man's own life? It is his basic possession, to retain or relinquish as he sees fit. If they continue to frustrate me, someone other than myself will suffer. I guarantee this.

My name is Henry Revere. My appearance is not remarkable, my intelligence is hardly noteworthy, and my emotions run evenly. I live in a house of synthetic shell, decorated with wood and jade, and surrounded by a pleasant garden. The view to one side is the ocean, to the other, a valley sprinkled with houses similar to my own. I am by no means a prisoner, although my servants supervise me with the most minute care. Their first concern is to prevent my suicide, just as mine is to achieve it.

It is a game in which they have all the advantages—a detailed knowledge of my psychology, corridors behind the walls from which they can observe me, and a host of technical devices. They are men of my own race, in fact of my own blood. But they are immeasurably more subtle than I.

My latest attempt was clever enough—although I had tried it before without success. I bit deeply into my tongue and thought to infect the cut with a pinch of garden loam. The servants either noticed me placing the soil in my mouth or observed the tension of my jaw.

They acted without warning. I stood on the terrace, hoping the soreness in my mouth might go undetected. Then, without conscious hiatus, I found myself reclining on a pallet, the dirt removed, the wound healed. They had used a thought-damping ray to anaesthetize me, and their sure medical techniques,

47

aided by my almost invulnerable constitution, defeated the scheme.

As usual, I concealed my annoyance and went to my study. This is a room I have designed to my own taste, as far as possible from the complex curvilinear style which expresses the spirit of the age.

Almost immediately the person in charge of the household entered the room. I call him Dr. Jones because I cannot pronounce his name. He is taller than I, slender and fine-boned. His features are small, beautifully shaped, except for his chin which to my mind is too sharp and long, although I understand that such a chin is a contemporary criterion of beauty. His eyes are very large, slightly protuberant; his skin is clean of hair, by reason both of the racial tendency toward hairlessness, and the depilation which every baby undergoes upon birth.

Dr. Jones' clothes are vastly fanciful. He wears a body mantle of green film and a dozen vari-colored disks which spin slowly around his body like an axis. The symbolism of these disks, with their various colors, patterns, and directions of spin, are discussed in a chapter of my *History of Man*—so I will not be discursive here. The disks serve also as gravity deflectors, and are used commonly in personal flight.

Dr. Jones made me a polite salute, and seated himself upon an invisible cushion of anti-gravity. He spoke in the contemporary speech, which I could understand well enough, but whose nasal trills, gutturals, sibilants and indescribable friccatives, I could never articulate.

"Well, Henry Revere, how goes it?" he asked.

In my pidgin-speech I made a noncommittal reply.

"I understand," said Dr. Jones, "that once again you undertook to deprive us of your company."

I nodded. "As usual I failed," I said.

Dr. Jones smiled slightly. The race had evolved away from laughter, which, as I understand, originated in the cave-man's bellow of relief at the successful clubbing of an adversary.

"You are self-centered," Dr. Jones told me. "You consider only your own pleasure."

"My life is my own. If I want to end it, you do great wrong in stopping me."

Dr. Jones shook his head. "But you are not your own property. You are the ward of the race. How much better if you accepted this fact!"

"I can't agree," I told him.

"It is necessary that you so adjust yourself." He studied me ruminatively. "You are something over ninety-six thousand years old. In my tenure at this house you have attempted suicide no less than a hundred times. No method has been either too crude or too painstaking."

He paused to watch me but I said nothing. He spoke no more than the truth, and for this reason I was allowed no object sharp enough to cut, long enough to strangle, noxious enough to poison, heavy enough to crush—even if I could have escaped surveillance long enough to use any deadly weapon.

I was ninety-six thousand, two hundred and thirty-two years old, and life long ago had lost that freshness and anticipation which makes it enjoyable. I found existence not so much unpleasant, as a bore. Events repeated themselves with a deadening familiarity. It was like watching a rather dull drama for the thousandth time: the boredom becomes almost tangible and nothing seems more desirable than oblivion.

Ninety-six thousand, two hundred and two years ago, as a student of bio-chemistry, I had offered myself as a guinea pig for certain tests involving glands and connective tissue. An incalculable error had distorted the experiment, with my immortality as the perverse result. To this day I appear not an hour older than my age at the time of the experiment, when I was so terribly young.

Needless to say, I suffered tragedy as my parents, my friends, my wife, and finally my children grew old and died, while I remained a young man. So it has been. I have seen untold generations come and go; faces flit before me like snowflakes as I sit here. Nations have risen and fallen, empires extended, collapsed, forgotten. Heroes have lived and died; seas drained, deserts irrigated, glaciers melted, mountains levelled. Almost a hundred thousand years I have persisted, for the most part effacing myself, studying humanity. My great work has been the *History of Man*.

Although I have lived unchanging, across the years the race evolved. Men and women grew taller, and more slender. Every century saw features more refined, brains larger, more flexible. As a result, I, Henry Revere, *homo sapiens* of the twentieth century, today am a freakish survival, somewhat more advanced than the Neanderthal, but essentially a precursor to the true Man of today.

I am a living fossil, a curio among curios, a public ward, a creature denied the option of life or death. This was what Dr.

Jones had come to explain to me, as if I were a retarded child. He was kindly, but unusually emphatic. Presently he departed and I was left to myself, in whatever privacy the scrutiny of half a dozen pairs of eyes allows.

It is harder to kill one's self than one might imagine. I have considered the matter carefully, examining every object within my control for lethal potentialities. But my servants are preternaturally careful. Nothing in this house could so much as bruise me. And when I leave the house, as I am privileged to do, gravity deflectors allow me no profit from high places, and in this exquisitely organized civilization there are no dangerous vehicles or heavy machinery in which I could mangle myself.

In the final analysis I am flung upon my own resources. I have an idea. Tonight I shall take a firm grasp on my head and try to break my neck ...

Dr. Jones came as always, and inspected me with his usual reproach. "Henry Revere, you trouble us all with your discontent. Why can't you reconcile yourself to life as you have always known it?"

"Because I am bored! I have experienced everything. There is no more possibility of novelty or surprise! I feel so sure of events that I could predict the future!"

He was rather more serious than usual. "You are our guest. You must realize that our only concern is to ensure your safety."

"But I don't want safety! Quite the reverse!"

Dr. Jones ignored me. "You must make up your mind to cooperate. Otherwise—" he paused significantly "—we will be forced into a course of action that will detract from the dignity of us all."

"Nothing could detract any further from my dignity," I replied bitterly. "I am hardly better than an animal in a zoo."

"That is neither your fault nor ours. We all must fulfill our existences to the optimum. Today your function is to serve as vinculum with the past."

He departed. I was left to my thoughts. The threats had been veiled but were all too clear. I was to desist from further attempts upon my life or suffer additional restraint.

I went out on the terrace, and stood looking across the ocean, where the sun was setting into a bed of golden clouds. I was beset by a dejection so vast that I felt stifled. Completely weary of a world to which I had become alien, I was yet denied freedom to take my leave. Everywhere I looked were avenues to death: the deep ocean, the heights of the palisade, the glitter of energy in the city. Death was a privilege, a bounty, a prize, and it was denied to me.

I returned to my study and leafed through some old maps. The house was silent—as if I were alone. I knew differently. Silent feet moved behind the walls, which were transparent to the eyes above these feet, but opaque to mine. Gauzy webs of artificial nerve tissue watched me from various parts of the room. I had only to make a sudden gesture to bring an anaesthetic beam snapping at me.

I sighed, slumped into my chair. I saw with the utmost clarity that never could I kill myself by my own instrumentality. Must I then submit to an intolerable existence? I sat looking bleakly at the nacreous wall behind which eyes noted my every act.

No, I would never submit. I must seek some means outside myself, a force of destruction to strike without warning: a lightning bolt, an avalanche, an earthquake.

Such natural cataclysms, however, were completely beyond my power to ordain or even predict.

I considered radioactivity. If by some pretext I could expose myself to a sufficient number of roentgens . . .

I sat back in my chair, suddenly excited. In the early days atomic wastes were sometimes buried, sometimes blended with concrete and dropped into the ocean. If only I were able to—but no. Dr. Jones would hardly allow me to dig in the desert or dive in the ocean, even if the radioactivity were not yet vitiated.

Some other disaster must be found in which I could serve the role of a casualty. If, for instance, I had foreknowledge of some great meteor, and where it would strike . . .

The idea awoke an almost forgotten association. I sat up in my chair. Then, conscious that knowledgeable minds speculated upon my every expression, I once again slumped forlornly.

Behind the passive mask of my face, my mind was racing, recalling ancient events. The time was too far past, the circumstances obscured. But details could be found in my great *History of Man*.

I must by all means avoid suspicion. I yawned, feigned acute ennui. Then with an air of surly petulance, I secured the box of numbered rods which was my index. I dropped one of them into the viewer, focused on the molecule-wide items of information.

Someone might be observing me. I rambled here and there, consulting articles and essays totally unrelated to my idea: *The Origin and Greatest Development of the Dithyramb; The Kalmuk Tyrants; New Camelot, 18119 A.D.; Oestheotics; The Caves of Phrygia; The Exploration of Mars; The Launching of the Satellites.* I undertook no more than a glance at this last; it would not be wise to show any more than a flicker of interest. But what I read corroborated the inkling which had tickled the back of my mind.

The date was during the twentieth century, during what would have been my normal lifetime.

The article read in part:

> Today HESPERUS, *last of the unmanned satellites was launched into orbit around Earth. This great machine will swing above the equator at a height of a thousand miles, where atmospheric resistance is so scant as to be negligible. Not quite negligible, of course; it is estimated that in something less than a hundred thousand years HESPERUS will lose enough momentum to return to Earth.*
>
> *Let us hope that no citizen of that future age suffers injury when HESPERUS falls.*

I grunted and muttered. A fatuous sentiment! Let us hope that one person, at the very least, suffers injury. Injury enough to erase him from life!

I continued to glance through the monumental work which had occupied so much of my time. I listened to aquaclave music from the old Poly-Pacific Empire; read a few pages from the Revolt of the Manitobans. Then, yawning and simulating hunger, I called for my evening meal.

Tomorrow I must locate more exact information, and brush up on orbital mathematics.

The *Hesperus* will drop into the Pacific Ocean at Latitude 0° 0′ 0.0″ ± 0.1″, Longitude 141° 12″ 63.9″ ± 0.2″, at 2 hours 22 minutes 18 seconds after standard noon on January 13 of next year. It will strike with a velocity of approximately one thousand miles an hour, and I hope to be on hand to absorb a certain percentage of its inertia.

I have been occupied seven months establishing these figures. Considering the necessary precautions, the dissimulation, the delicacy of the calculations, seven months is a short time to accomplish as much as I have. I see no reason why my calculations should not be accurate. The basic data were recorded to the necessary refinement and there have been no variables or fluctuations to cause error.

I have considered light pressure, hysteresis, meteoric dust; I have reckoned the calendar reforms which have occurred over the years; I have allowed for any possible Einsteinian, Gambade, or Bolbinski perturbation. What is there left to disturb the *Hesperus*? Its orbit lies in the equatorial plane, south of spaceship channels; to all intents and purposes it has been forgotten.

The last mention of the *Hesperus* occurs about eleven thousand years after it was launched. I find a note to the effect that its orbital position and velocity were in exact accordance with theoretical values. I believe I can be certain that the *Hesperus* will fall on schedule.

The most cheerful aspect to the entire affair is that no one is aware of the impending disaster but myself.

The date is *January 9*. To every side long blue swells are rolling, rippled with cat's-paws. Above are blue skies and dazzling white clouds. The yacht slides quietly southwest in the general direction of the Marquesas Islands.

Dr. Jones had no enthusiasm for this cruise. At first he tried to dissuade me from what he considered a whim but I insisted, reminding him that I was theoretically a free man and he made no further difficulty.

The yacht is graceful, swift, and seems as fragile as a moth. But when we cut through the long swells there is no shudder or vibration—only a gentle elastic heave. If I had hoped to lose myself overboard, I would have suffered disappointment. I am shephereded as carefully as in my own house. But for the first time in many years I am relaxed and happy. Dr. Jones notices and approves.

The weather is beautiful—the water so blue, the sun so bright, the air so fresh that I almost feel a qualm at leaving this life. Still, now is my chance and I must seize it. I regret that Dr. Jones and the crew must die with me. Still—what do they lose? Very little. A few short years. This is the risk they assume when they guard me. If I could allow them survival I would do so—but there is no such possibility.

I have requested and have been granted nominal command of the yacht. That is to say, I plot the course, I set the speed. Dr. Jones looks on with indulgent amusement, pleased that I interest myself in matters outside myself.

*January 12.* Tomorrow is my last day of life. We passed through a series of rain squalls this morning, but the horizon ahead is clear. I expect good weather tomorrow.

I have throttled down to Dead-Slow, as we are only a few hundred miles from our destination.

*January 13.* I am tense, active, charged with vitality and awareness. Every part of me tingles. On this day of my death it is good to be alive. And why? Because of anticipation, eagerness, hope.

I am trying to mask my euphoria. Dr. Jones is extremely sensitive; I would not care to start his mind working at this late date.

The time is noon. I keep my appointment with *Hesperus* in two hours and twenty-two minutes. The yacht is coasting easily over the water. Our position, as recorded by a pin-point of light on the chart, is only a few miles from our final position. At this present rate we will arrive in about two hours and fifteen minutes. Then I will halt the yacht and wait . . .

The yacht is motionless on the ocean. Our position is exactly at Latitude 0° 0′ 0.0″, Longitude 141° 12″ 63.9″. The degree of error represents no more than a yard or two. This graceful yacht with the unpronounceable name sits directly on the bull's eye. There is only five minutes to wait.

Dr. Jones comes into the cabin. He inspects me curiously. "You seem very keyed up, Henry Revere."

"Yes, I feel keyed up, stimulated. This cruise is affording me much pleasure."

"Excellent!" He walks to the chart, glances at it. "Why are we halted?"

"I took it into my mind to drift quietly. Are you impatient?"

Time passes—minutes, seconds. I watch the chronometer. Dr. Jones follows my glance. He frowns in sudden recollection, goes to the telescreen. "Excuse me; something I would like to watch. You might be interested."

The screen depicts an arid waste. "The Kalahari Desert," Dr. Jones tells me. "Watch."

I glance at the chronometer. Ten seconds—they tick off. Five—four—three—two—one. A great whistling sound, a roar, a crash, an explosion! It comes from the telescreen. The yacht rides on a calm sea.

"There went *Hesperus*," said Dr. Jones. "Right on schedule!"

He looks at me, where I have sagged against a bulkhead. His eyes narrow, he looks at the chronometer, at the chart, at the telescreen, back to me. "Ah, I understand you now! All of us you would have killed!"

"Yes," I mutter, "all of us."

"Aha! You savage!"

I pay him no heed. "Where could I have miscalculated? I considered everything. Loss of entropic mass, lunar attractions—I know the orbit of *Hesperus* as I know my hand. How did it shift, and so far?"

Dr. Jones eyes shine with a baleful light. "You know the orbit of *Hesperus* then?"

"Yes. I considered every aspect."

"And you believe it shifted?"

"It must have. It was launched into an equatorial orbit; it falls into the Kalahari."

"There are two bodies to be considered."

"Two?"

"*Hesperus* and Earth."

"Earth is constant . . . Unchangeable." I say this last word slowly, as the terrible knowledge comes.

And Dr. Jones, for the first time in my memory, laughs, an unpleasant harsh sound. "Constant—unchangeable. Except for libration of the poles. *Hesperus* is the constant. Earth shifts below."

"Yes! What a fool I am!"

"An insensate murdering fool! I see you cannot be trusted!"

I charge him. I strike him once in the face before the anaesthetic beam hits me.

# The World-Thinker

## 1

Through the open window came sounds of the city—the swish of passing air traffic, the clank of the pedestrian belt on the ramp below, hoarse undertones from the lower levels. Cardale sat by the window studying a sheet of paper which displayed a photograph and a few lines of type:

### FUGITIVE!

Isabel May—Age 21; height 5 feet 5 inches; medium physique.
> Hair: black (could be dyed).
> Eyes: blue.
> Distinguishing characteristics: none.

Cardale shifted his eyes to the photograph and studied the pretty face with incongruously angry eyes. A placard across her chest read: *94E-627.* Cardale returned to the printed words.

> Sentenced to serve three years at the Nevada
> Women's Camp, in the first six months of
> incarceration Isabel May accumulated 22 months
> additional punitive confinement. Caution is
> urged in her apprehension.

The face, Cardale reflected, was defiant, reckless, outraged, but neither coarse nor stupid—a face, in fact, illuminated by intelligence and sensitivity. Not the face of a criminal, thought Cardale.

He pressed a button. The telescreen plumbed into sharp life. "Lunar Observatory," said Cardale.

The screen twitched to a view across an austere office, with moonscape outside the window. A man in a rose-pink smock looked into the screen. "Hello, Cardale."

"What's the word on May?"

"We've got a line on her. Quite a nuisance, which you won't want to hear about. One matter: please, in the future, keep freighters in another sector when you want a fugitive tracked. We had six red herrings to cope with."

"But you picked up May?"

"Definitely."

"Keep her in your sights. I'll send someone out to take over." Cardale clicked off the screen.

He ruminated a moment, then summoned the image of his secretary. "Get me Detering at Central Intelligence."

The polychrome whirl of color rose and fell to reveal Detering's ruddy face.

"Cardale, if it's service you want—"

"I want a mixed squad, men and women, in a fast ship to pick up a fugitive. Her name is Isabel May. She's fractious, unruly, incorrigible—but I don't want her hurt."

"Allow me to continue what I started to say. Cardale, if you want service, you are out of luck. There's literally no one in the office but me."

"Then come yourself."

"To pick up a reckless woman, and get my hair pulled and my face slapped? No thanks . . . One moment. There's a man waiting outside my office on a disciplinary charge. I can either have him court-martialed or I can send him over to you."

"What's his offense?"

"Insubordination. Arrogance. Disregard of orders. He's a loner. He does as he pleases and to hell with the rule book."

"What about results?"

"He gets results—of a sort. His own kind of results."

"He may be the man to bring back Isabel May. What's his name?"

"Lanarck. He won't use his rank, which is captain."

"He seems something of a free spirit. . . . Well, send him over."

Lanarck arrived almost immediately. The secretary ushered him into Cardale's office.

"Sit down, please. My name is Cardale. You're Lanarck, right?"

"Quite right."

Cardale inspected his visitor with open curiosity. Lanarck's reputation, thought Cardale, was belied by his appearance. He was neither tall nor heavy, and carried himself unobtrusively. His features, deeply darkened by the hard waves of space, were regular and dominated by a cold directness of the gray eyes and a bold jutting nose. Lanarck's voice was pleasant and soft.

"Major Detering assigned me to you for orders, sir."

"He recommended you highly," said Cardale. "I have a ticklish job on hand. Look at this." He passed over the sheet with the photograph of Isabel May. Lanarck scrutinized it without comment and handed it back.

"This girl was imprisoned six months ago for assault with a deadly weapon. She escaped the day before yesterday into space—which is more or less trivial in itself. But she carries with her a quantity of important information, which must be retrieved for the economic well-being of Earth. This may seem to you an extravagant statement, but accept it from me as a fact."

Lanarck said in a patient voice: "Mr. Cardale, I find that I work most efficiently when I am equipped with facts. Give me details of the case. If you feel that the matter is too sensitive for my handling, I will retire and you may bring in operatives better qualified."

Cardale said crossly: "The girl's father is a high-level mathematician, at work for the Exchequer. By his instruction an elaborate method of security to regulate transfer of funds was evolved. As an emergency precaution he devised an over-ride system, consisting of several words in a specific sequence. A criminal could go to the telephone, call the Exchequer, use these words and direct by voice alone the transfer of a billion dollars to his personal account. Or a hundred billion."

"Why not cancel the over-ride and install another?"

"Because of Arthur May's devilish subtlety. The over-ride is hidden in the computer; it is buried, totally inaccessible, that it might be protected from someone ordering the computer to reveal the over-ride. The only way the over-ride can be voided is to use the over-ride first and issue appropriate orders."

"Go on."

"Arthur May knew the over-ride. He agreed to transfer the knowledge to the Chancellor and then submit to a hypnotic process which would remove the knowledge from his brain. Now occurred a rather sordid matter in regard to May's remuneration, and in my mind he was absolutely in the right."

"I know the feeling," said Lanarck. "I've had my own troubles with the scoundrels. The only good bursar is a dead bursar."

"In any event there follows an incredible tale of wrangling, proposals, estimates, schemes, counter-proposals, counter-schemes and conniving, all of which caused Arthur May a mental breakdown and he forgot the over-ride. But he had anticipated something of the sort and he left a memorandum with his daughter: Isabel May. When the authorities came for her father, she refused to let them in; she performed violent acts; she was confined in a penal institution, from which she escaped. Regardless of rights and wrongs she must be captured, more or less gently, and brought back—with the over-ride. You will surely understand the implications of the situation."

"It is a complicated business," said Lanarck. "But I will go after the girl, and with luck I will bring her back."

Six hours later Lanarck arrived at Lunar Observatory. The in-iris expanded; the boat lurched through.

Inside the dome Lanarck unclamped the port, stepped out. The master astronomer approached. Behind came the mechanics, one of whom bore an instrument which they welded to the hull of Lanarck's spaceboat.

"It's a detector cell," the astronomer explained. "Right now it's holding a line on the ship you're to follow. When the indicator holds to the neutral zone, you're on her track."

"And where does this ship seem to be headed?"

The astronomer shrugged. "Nowhere in tellurian space. She's way past Fomalhaut and lining straight out."

Lanarck stood silent. This was hostile space Isabel May was entering. In another day or so she would be slicing the fringe of the Clantlalan System, where the space patrol of that dark and inimical empire without warning destroyed all approaching vessels. Further on opened a region of black stars, inhabited by nondescript peoples little better than pirates. Still farther beyond lay unexplored and consequently dangerous regions.

The mechanics were finished. Lanarck climbed back into the boat. The out-iris opened; he drove his craft through, down the runway, and off into space.

A slow week followed, in which distance was annihilated. Earth empire fell far astern: a small cluster of stars. To one side the Clantlalan System grew ever brighter, and as Lanarck passed by, the Clantlalan space-spheres tried to close with him. He threw in the emergency bank of generators and whisked the warboat far ahead. Someday, Lanarck knew, he would slip down past the guard ships to the home planet by the twin red suns, to discover what secret was held so dear. But now he kept the detector centered in the dial, and day by day the incoming signals from his quarry grew stronger.

They passed through the outlaw-ridden belt of dark stars, and into a region of space unknown but for tales let slip by drunken Clantlalan renegades—reports of planets covered with mighty ruins, legends of an asteroid littered with a thousand wrecked spaceships. Other tales were even more incredible. A dragon who tore spaceships open in its jaws purportedly wandered through this region, and it was said that alone on a desolate planet a godlike being created worlds at his pleasure.

The signals in the detector cell presently grew so strong that Lanarck slackened speed for fear that, overshooting his quarry, the cell would lose its thread of radiation. Now Isabel May began to swing out toward the star-systems which drifted past like fireflies, as if she sought a landmark. Always the signals in the detector cell grew stronger.

A yellow star waxed bright ahead. Lanarck knew that the ship of Isabel May was close at hand. Into that yellow star's system he followed her, and lined out the trail toward the single planet. Presently, as the planet globed out before him, the signals ceased entirely.

The high clear atmosphere braked the motion of Lanarck's space-boat. He found below a dun, sun-baked landscape. Through the telescope the surface appeared to be uniformly stony and flat. Clouds of dust indicated the presence of high winds.

He had no trouble finding Isabel May's ship. In the field of his telescope lay a cubical white building: the only landmark visible from horizon to horizon. Beside the building sat Isabel May's silver spaceboat. Lanarck swooped to a landing, half expecting a bolt from her needle-beam. The port of the spaceboat hung open, but she did not show herself as he came down on his crash-keel close by.

The air, he found, was breathable. Buckling on his needle-beam, he stepped out on the stony ground. The hot gale tore at him, buffeting his face, whipping tears from his eyes. Wind-flung pebbles bounding along the ground stung his legs. Light from the sun burned his shoulders.

Lanarck inspected the terrain, to discover no sign of life, either from the white building or from Isabel May's spaceboat. The ground stretched away, bare and sun-drenched, far into the dusty distances. Lanarck looked to the lonely white structure. She must be within. Here was the end of the chase which had brought him across the galaxy.

## 2

Lanarck circled the building. On the leeward side he found a low dark archway. From within came the heavy smell of life: an odor half animal, half reptile. He approached the entrance with his needle-beam ready.

He called out: "Isabel May!" He listened. The wind whistled by the corner of the building; little stones clicked past, blowing down the endless sun-dazzled waste. There was no other sound.

A sonorous voice entered his brain.

"The one you seek is gone."

Lanarck stood stock-still.

"You may come within, Earthman. We are not enemies."

The archway loomed dark before him. Step by step he entered. After the glare of the white sun the dimness of the room was like a moonless night. Lanarck blinked.

Slowly objects about him assumed form. Two enormous eyes peered through the gloom; behind appeared a tremendous domelike bulk. Thought surged into Lanarck's brain. "You are unnecessarily truculent. Here will be no occasion for violence."

Lanarck relaxed, feeling slightly at a loss. Telepathy was not often practiced upon Earth. The creature's messages came like a paradoxically silent voice, but he had no knowledge how to transmit his own messages. He hazarded the experiment.

"Where is Isabel May?"

"In a place inaccessible to you."

"How did she go? Her spaceboat is outside, and she landed but a half-hour ago."

"I sent her away."

Keeping his needle-beam ready, Lanarck searched the building. The girl was nowhere to be found. Seized by a sudden fearful thought, he ran to the entrance and looked out. The two spaceboats were as he had left them. He shoved the needle-beam back into the holster and turned to the leviathan, in whom he sensed benign amusement.

"Well, then—who are you and where is Isabel May?"

"I am Laoome," came the reply. "Laoome, the one-time Third of Narfilhet—Laoome the World-Thinker, the Final Sage of the Fifth Universe . . . As for the girl, I have placed her, at her own request, upon a pleasant but inaccessible world of my own creation."

Lanarck stood perplexed.

"Look!" Laoome said.

Space quivered in front of Lanarck's eyes. A dark aperture appeared in midair. Looking through, Lanarck saw hanging apparently but a yard before his eyes a lambent sphere—a miniature world. As he watched, it expanded like a toy balloon.

Its horizons vanished past the confines of the opening. Continents and oceans assumed shape, flecked with cloud-wisps. Polar ice caps glinted blue-white in the light of an unseen sun. Yet all the time the world seemed to be but a yard distant. A plain appeared, rimmed by black, flinty mountains. The color of the plain, a ruddy ocher, he saw presently, was due to a forest carpet of rust-colored foliage. The expansion ceased.

The World-Thinker spoke: "That which you see before you is matter as real and tangible as yourself. I have indeed created it through my mind. Until I dissolve it in the same manner, it exists. Reach out and touch it."

Lanarck did so. It was actually only a yard from his face, and the red forest crushed like dry moss under his fingertips.

"You destroyed a village," commented Laoome, and caused the world to expand once more at a breathtaking rate, until the perspectives were as if Lanarck hung a hundred feet above the surface. He was looking into the devastation which his touch had wrought a moment before. The trees, far larger than he had supposed, with boles thirty or forty feet through, lay tossed and shattered. Visible were the ruins of rude huts, from which issued calls and screams of pain, thinly audible to Lanarck. Bodies of men and women lay crushed. Others tore frantically at the wreckage.

Lanarck stared in disbelief. "There's life! Men!"

"Without life, a world is uninteresting, a lump of rock. Men, like yourself, I often use. They have a large capacity for emotion and initiative, a flexibility to the varied environments which I introduce."

Lanarck gazed at the tips of his fingers, then back to the shattered village. "Are they really alive?"

"Certainly. And you would find, should you converse with one of them, that they possess a sense of history, a racial heritage of folklore, and a culture well-adapted to their environment."

"But how can one brain conceive the detail of a world? The leaves of each tree, the features of each man—"

"That would be tedious," Laoome agreed. "My mind only broadly conceives, introduces the determinate roots into the hypostatic equations. Detail then evolves automatically."

"You allowed me to destroy hundreds of these—men."

Curious feelers searched his brain. Lanarck sensed Laoome's amusement.

"The idea is repugnant? In a moment I shall dissolve the entire world. . . . Still, if it pleases you, I can restore it as it was. See!"

Immediately the forest was unmarred, the village whole again, secure and peaceful in a small clearing.

Awareness came to Lanarck of a curious rigidity in the rapport he had established with the World-Thinker. Looking about, he saw that the great eyes had glazed, that the tremendous black body was twitching and jerking. Now Laoome's dream-planet was changing. Lanarck leaned forward in fascination. The noble red trees had become gray rotten stalks and were swaying drunkenly. Others slumped and folded like columns of putty.

On the ground balls of black slime rolled about with vicious energy pursuing the villagers, who in terror fled anywhere, everywhere.

From the heavens came a rain of blazing pellets. The villagers were killed, but the black slime-things seemed only agonized. Blindly they lashed about, burrowed furiously into the heaving ground to escape the impacts. More suddenly than it had been created, the world vanished. Lanarck tore his gaze from the spot where the world had been. He looked about and found Laoome as before.

"Don't be alarmed." The thoughts came quietly. "The seizure is over. It occurs only seldom, and why it should be I do not know. I imagine that my brain, under the pressure of exact thought, lapses into these reflexive spasms for the sake of relaxation. This was a mild attack. The world on which I am concentrating is usually totally destroyed."

The flow of soundless words stopped abruptly. Moments passed. Then thoughts gushed once more into Lanarck's brain.

"Let me show you another planet—one of the most interesting I have ever conceived. For almost a million Earth years it has been developing in my mind."

The space before Lanarck's eyes quivered. Out in the imaginary void hung another planet. As before, it expanded until the features of the terrain assumed an earthly perspective. Hardly a mile in diameter, the world was divided around the equator by a belt of sandy desert. At one pole glimmered a lake, at the other grew a jungle of lush vegetation.

From this jungle now, as Lanarck watched, crept a semi-human shape. A travesty upon man, its face was long, chinless and furtive, with eyes beady and quick. The legs were unnaturally long; the shoulders and arms were undeveloped. It slunk to the edge of the desert, paused a moment, looking carefully in both directions, then began a mad dash through the sand to the lake beyond.

Halfway across, a terrible roar was heard. Over the close horizon bounded a dragonlike monster. With fearsome speed it pursued the fleeing man-thing, who outdistanced it and gained the edge of the desert by two hundred feet. When the dragon came to the limits of the sandy area, it halted and bellowed an eerie mournful note which sent shivers along Lanarck's spine. Casually now, the man-thing loped to the lake, threw himself flat and drank deeply.

"An experiment in evolution," came Laoome's thought. "A million years ago those creatures were men like yourself. This world is oddly designed. At one end is food, at the other drink. In order to survive, the 'men' must cross the desert every day or so. The dragon is prevented from leaving the desert by actinic boundaries. Hence, if the men can cross the desert, they are safe.

"You have witnessed how admirably they have adapted to their environment. The women are particularly fleet, for they have adjusted to the handicap of caring for their young. Sooner or later, of course, age overtakes them and their speed gradually decreases until finally they are caught and devoured.

"A curious religion and set of taboos have evolved here. I

am worshipped as the primary god of Life, and Shillal, as they call the dragon, is the deity of Death. He, of course, is the basic concern of their lives and colors all their thoughts. They are close to elementals, these folk. Food, drink, and death are intertwined for them into almost one concept.

"They can build no weapons of metal against Shillal, for their world is not endowed with the raw materials. Once, a hundred thousand years ago, one of their chiefs contrived a gigantic catapult, to hurl a sharp-pointed tree trunk at Shillal. Unluckily, the fibers of the draw-cord snapped and the chief was killed by the recoil. The priests interpreted this as a sign and—"

"Look there! Shillal catches a weary old woman, sodden with water, attempting to return to the jungle!"

Lanarck witnessed the beast's great gulping.

"To continue," Laoome went on, "a taboo was created, and no further weapons were ever built."

"But why have you forced upon these folk a million years of wretched existence?" asked Lanarck.

Laoome gave an untranslatable mental shrug. "I am just, and indeed benevolent," he said. "These men worship me as a god. Upon a certain hillock, which they hold sacred, they bring their sick and wounded. There, if the whim takes me, I restore them to health. So far as their existence is concerned, they relish the span of their lives as much as you do yours."

"Yet, in creating these worlds, you are responsible for the happiness of the inhabitants. If you were truly benevolent, why should you permit disease and terror to exist?"

Laoome again gave his mental shrug. "I might say that I use this universe of our own as a model. Perhaps there is another Laoome dreaming out the worlds we ourselves live on. When man dies of sickness, bacteria live. Dragon lives by eating man. When man eats, plants and animals die."

Lanarck was silent, studiously preventing his thoughts from rising to the surface of his mind.

"I take it that Isabel May is upon neither of these planets?"

"That is correct."

"I ask that you make it possible for me to communicate with her."

"But I put her upon a world expressly to assure her safety from such molestation."

"I believe that she would profit by hearing me."

"Very well," said Laoome. "In justice I should accord to you the same opportunity that I did her. You may proceed to this world. Remember, however, the risk is your own, exactly as it is for Isabel May. If you perish upon Markavvel, you are as thoroughly dead as you might be upon Earth. I can not play Destiny to influence either one of your lives."

There was hiatus in Laoome's thoughts, a whirl of ideas too rapid for Lanarck to grasp. At last Laoome's eyes focused upon him again. An instant of faintness as Lanarck felt knowledge forced into his brain.

As Laoome silently regarded him, it occurred to Lanarck that Laoome's body, a great dome of black flesh, was singularly ill-adapted to life on the planet where he dwelt.

"You are right," came the thoughts of Laoome. "From a Beyond unknown to you I came, banished from the dark planet Narfilhet, in whose fathomless black waters I swam. This was long ago, but even now I may not return." Laoome lapsed once more into introspection.

Lanarck moved restlessly. Outside the wind tore past the building. Laoome continued silent, dreaming perhaps of the dark oceans of ancient Narfilhet. Lanarck impatiently launched a thought.

"How do I reach Markavvel? And how do I return?"

Laoome fetched himself back to the present. His eyes settled upon a point beside Lanarck. The aperture which led into his various imaginary spaces was now wrenched open for the third time. A little distance off in the void, a spaceboat drifted. Lanarck's eyes narrowed with sudden interest.

"That's a 45-G—my own ship!" he exclaimed.

"No, not yours. One like it. Yours is still outside." The craft drew nearer, gradually floated within reach.

"Climb in," said Laoome. "At present Isabel May is in the city which lies at the apex of the triangular continent."

"But how do I get back?"

"Aim your ship, when you leave Markavvel, at the brightest star visible. You will then break through the mental dimensions into this universe."

Lanarck reached his arm into the imaginary universe and pulled the imagined space-boat close to the aperture. He opened the port and gingerly stepped in as Laoome's parting thoughts reached him.

"Should you fall into danger, I can not modify the natural course of events. On the other hand, I will not intentionally place dangers in your way. If such befall you, it will be due solely to circumstance."

## 3

Lanarck slammed shut the port, half expecting the ship to dissolve under his feet. But the ship was solid enough. He looked back. The gap into his own universe had disappeared, leaving in its place a brilliant blue star. He found himself in space. Below glimmered the disk of Markavvel, much like other planets he had approached from the void. He tugged at the throttle, threw the nose hard over and down. Let the abstracts take care for themselves. The boat dropped down at Markavvel.

It seemed a pleasant world. A hot white sun hung off in space; blue oceans covered a large part of the surface. Among the scattered land masses he found the triangular continent. It was not large. There were mountains with green-forested slopes and a central plateau: a not un-Earth-like scene, and Lanarck did not feel the alien aura which surrounded most extraterrestrial planets.

Sighting through his telescope Lanarck found the city, sprawling and white, at the mouth of a wide river. He sent his ship streaking down through the upper atmosphere, then slowed and leveled off thirty miles to sea. Barely skimming the sparkling blue waves, he flew toward the city.

A few miles to the left an island raised basalt cliffs against the ocean. In his line of sight there heaved up on the crest of a swell a floating black object. After an instant it disappeared into the trough: a ramshackle raft. Upon it a girl with tawny golden hair desperately battled sea-things which sought to climb aboard.

Lanarck dropped the ship into the water beside the raft. The wash threw the raft up and over and down on the girl.

Lanarck slipped through the port and dived into clear green water. He glimpsed only sub-human figures paddling downward, barely discernible. Bobbing to the surface, he swam to the raft, ducked under, grasped the girl's limp form, pulled her into the air.

For a moment he clung to the raft to catch his breath, while holding the girl's head clear of the water. He sensed the return of the creatures from below. Dark forms rose in the shadow cast by the raft, and a clammy, long-fingered hand wound around his ankle. He kicked and felt his foot thud into something like a face. More dark forms came up from the depths. Lanarck measured the distance to his spaceboat. Forty feet. Too far. He crawled onto the raft, and pulled the girl after him. Leaning far out, he recovered the paddle and prepared to smash the first sea-thing to push above water. But instead, they swam in tireless circles twenty feet below.

The blade of the paddle had broken, Lanarck could not move the unwieldly bulk of the raft. The breeze, meanwhile, was easing the spaceboat even farther away. Lanarck exerted himself another fifteen minutes, pushing against the water with the splintered paddle, but the gap increased. He cast down the paddle in disgust and turned to the girl, who, sitting cross-legged, regarded him thoughtfully. For no apparent reason, Lanarck was reminded of Laoome in the dimness of his white building, on the windy world. All this, he thought, looking from clear-eyed girl to heaving sun-lit sea to highlands of the continent ahead, was an idea in Laoome's brain.

He looked back at the girl. Her bright wheat-colored hair frothed around her head in ringlets, producing, thought Lanarck, a most pleasant effect. She returned his gaze for a moment, then, with jaunty grace, stood up.

She spoke to Lanarck who found to his amazement that he understood her. Then, remembering Laoome's manipulation of his brain, extracting ideas, altering, instilling new concepts, he was not so amazed.

"Thank you for your help," she said. "But now we are both in the same plight."

Lanarck said nothing. He knelt and began to remove his boots.

"What will you do?"

"Swim," he answered. The new language seemed altogether natural.

"The Bottom-people would pull you under before you went twenty feet." She pointed into the water, which teemed with circling dark shapes. Lanarck knew she spoke the truth.

"You are of Earth also?" she asked, inspecting him carefully.

"Yes. Who are you and what do you know of Earth?"

"I am Jiro from the city yonder, which is Gahadion. Earth is the home of Isabel May, who came in a ship such as yours."

"Isabel May arrived but an hour ago! How could you know about her?"

"An hour?" replied the girl. "She has been here three months!" This last a little bitterly.

Lanarck reflected that Laoome controlled time in his universes as arbitrarily as he did space. "How did you come to be here on this raft?"

She grimaced toward the island. "The priests came for me. They live on the island and take people from the mainland. They took me but last night I escaped."

Lanarck looked from the island to the city on the mainland. "Why do not Gahadion authorities control the priests?"

Her lips rounded to an O. "They are sacred to the Great God Laoome, and so inviolate."

Lanarck wondered what unique evolutionary process Laoome had in progress here.

"Few persons thus taken return to the mainland," she went on. "Those who win free, and also escape the Bottom-people, usually live in the wilderness. If they return to Gahadion they are molested by fanatics and sometimes recaptured by the priests."

Lanarck was silent. After all, it concerned him little how these people fared. They were beings of fantasy, inhabiting an imaginary planet. And yet, when he looked at Jiro, detachment became easier to contemplate than to achieve.

"And Isabel May is in Gahadion?"

Jiro's lips tightened. "No. She lives on the island. She is the Thrice-Adept, the High Priestess."

Lanarck was surprised. "Why did they make her High Priestess?"

"A month after she arrived, the Hierarch, learning of the woman whose hair was the color of night, even as yours, tried to take her to Drefteli, the Sacred Isle, as a slave. She killed him with her weapon. Then when the lightnings of Laoome did not consume her, it was known that Laoome approved, and so she was made High Priestess in place of the riven Hierarch."

The philosophy, so Lanarck reflected, would have sounded naïve on Earth, where the gods were more covert in their supervision of human affairs.

"Is Isabel May a friend of yours—or your lover?" asked Jiro softly.

"Hardly."

"Then what do you want with her?"

"I've come to take her back to Earth." He looked dubiously across the ever-widening gap between the raft and his spaceboat. "That at least was my intention."

"You shall see her soon," said Jiro. She pointed to a long black galley approaching from the island. "The Ordained Ones. I am once more a slave."

"Not yet," said Lanarck, feeling for the bulk of his needle-beam.

The galley, thrust by the force of twenty long oars, lunged toward them. On the after-deck stood a young woman, her black hair blowing in the wind. As her features became distinct, Lanarck recognized the face of Cardale's photograph, now serene and confident.

Isabel May, looking from the silent two on the raft to the wallowing spaceboat a quarter-mile distant, seemed to laugh. The galley, manned by tall, golden-haired men, drew alongside.

"So Earth Intelligence pays me a visit?" She spoke in English. "How you found me, I cannot guess." She looked curiously at Lanarck's somber visage. "How?"

"I followed your trail, and then explained the situation to Laoome."

"Just what is the situation?"

"I'd like to work out some kind of compromise to please everyone."

"I don't care whether I please anyone or not."

"Understandable."

The two studied each other. Isabel May suddenly asked, "What is your name?"

"Lanarck."

"Just Lanarck? No rank? No first name?"

"Lanarck is enough."

"Just as you like. I hardly know what to do with you. I'm not vindictive, and I don't want to handicap your career. But ferrying you to your spaceboat would be rather quixotic. I'm comfortable here, and I haven't the slightest intention of turning my property over to you."

Lanarck reached for his needle-beam.

She watched him without emotion. "Wet needle-beams don't work well."

"This one is the exception." Lanarck blasted the figurehead from the galley.

Isabel May's expression changed suddenly. "I see that I'm wrong. How did you do it?"

"A personal device," replied Lanarck. "Now I'll have to request that you take me to my spaceboat."

Isabel May stared at him a moment, and in those blue eyes Lanarck detected something familiar. Where had he seen eyes with that expression? On Fan, the Pleasure Planet? In the Magic Groves of Hycithil? During the raids on the slave pens of Starlen? In Earth's own macropolis Tran?

She turned and muttered to her boatswain, a bronzed giant, his golden hair bound back by a copper band. He bowed and moved away.

"Very well," said Isabel May. "Come aboard."

Jiro and Lanarck clambered over the carven gunwale. The galley swept ahead, foaming up white in its wake.

Isabel May turned her attention to Jiro, who sat looking disconsolately toward the island Drefteli. "You make friends quickly," Isabel told Lanarck. "She's very beautiful. What are you planning for her?"

"She's one of your escaped slaves. I don't have any plans. This place belongs to Laoome; he makes all plans. I'm interested only in getting you out. If you don't want to come back to Earth, give me the document which you brought with you, and stay here as long as you like."

"Sorry. The document stays with me. I don't carry it on my person, so please don't try to search me."

"That sounds quite definite," said Lanarck. "Do you know what's in the document?"

"More or less. It's like a blank check on the wealth of the world."

"That's a good description. As I understand this sorry affair, you became angry at the treatment accorded your father."

"That's a very quiet understatement."

"Would money help soothe your anger?"

"I don't want money. I want revenge. I want to grind faces into the mud; I want to kick people and make their lives miserable."

"Still don't dismiss money. It's nice to be rich. You have your life ahead of you. I don't imagine you want to spend it here, inside Laoome's head."

"Very true."

"So name a figure."

"I can't measure anger and grief in dollars."

"Why not? A million? Ten million? A hundred million?"

"Stop there. I can't count any higher."

"That's your figure."

"What good will money do me? They'll take me back to Nevada."

"No. I'll give you my personal guarantee of this."

"Meaningless. I know nothing about you."

"You'll learn during the trip back to Earth."

Isabel May said: "Lanarck, you are persuasive. If the truth be known, I'm homesick." She turned away and stood looking over the ocean. Lanarck stood watching her. She was undeniably attractive and he found it difficult to take his eyes from her. But as he settled on the bench beside Jiro, he felt a surge of a different, stronger, feeling. It irritated him, and he tried to put it aside.

## 4

Wallowing in the swells, the spaceboat lay dead ahead. The galley scudded through the water at a great rate, and the oarsmen did not slacken speed as they approached. Lanarck's eyes narrowed; he jumped upright shouting orders. The galley, unswerving, plowed into the spaceboat, grinding it under the metal-shod keel. Water gushed in through the open port; the spaceboat shuddered and sank, a dark shadow plummeting into green depths.

"Too bad," remarked Isabel. "On the other hand, this puts us more on an equal footing. You have a needle-beam, I have a spaceboat."

Lanarck silently seated himself. After a moment he spoke. "Where is your own needle-beam?"

"I blew it up trying to recharge it from the spaceboat generators."

"And where is your spaceboat?"

Isabel laughed at this. "Do you expect me to tell you?"

"Why not? I wouldn't maroon you here."

"Nevertheless, I don't think I'll tell you."

Lanarck turned to Jiro. "Where is Isabel May's spaceboat?"

Isabel spoke in a haughty voice: "As High Priestess to Almighty Laoome, I command you to be silent!"

Jiro looked from one to the other. She made up her mind. "It is on the plaza of the Malachite Temple in Gahadion."

Isabel was silent. "Laoome plays tricks," she said at last.

"Jiro has taken a fancy to you. You're obviously interested in her."

"Laoome will not interfere," said Lanarck.

She laughed bitterly. "That's what he told me—and look! I'm High Priestess. He also told me he wouldn't let anyone come to Markavvel from the outside to molest me. But you are here!"

"My intention is not to molest you," said Lanarck curtly. "We can as easily be friends as enemies."

"I don't care to be a friend of yours. And as an enemy, you are no serious problem. Now!" Isabel called, as the tall boatswain came near.

The boatswain whirled on Lanarck. Lanarck twisted, squirmed, heaved, and the golden-haired boatswain sprawled back into the bilge, where he lay dazed.

A soft hand brushed Lanarck's thigh. He looked around, smoothing his lank black hair, and found Isabel May smiling into his face. His needle-beam dangled from her fingers.

Jiro arose from the bench. Before Isabel could react, Jiro had pushed a hand into her face, and with the other seized the needle-beam. She pointed the weapon at Isabel.

"Sit down," said Jiro.

Weeping with rage, Isabel fell back upon the bench.

Jiro, her young face flushed and happy, backed over to the thwart, needle-beam leveled.

Lanarck stood still.

"I will take charge now," said Jiro. "You—Isabel! Tell your men to row toward Gahadion!"

Sullenly Isabel gave the order. The long black galley turned its bow toward the city.

"This may be sacrilege," Jiro observed to Lanarck. "But then I was already in trouble for escaping from Drefteli."

"What do you plan in this new capacity of yours?" Lanarck inquired, moving closer.

"First, to try this weapon on whomever thinks he can take it away from me." Lanarck eased back. "Secondly—but you'll see soon enough."

White-tiered Gahadion rapidly drew closer across the water.

Isabel sulked on the bench. Lanarck had little choice but to let matters move on their own momentum. He relaxed against a thwart, watching Jiro from the corner of his eye. She stood erect behind the bench where Isabel sat, her clear eyes looking over the leaping sparkles of the ocean. Breeze whipped her hair behind and pressed the tunic against her slim body. Lanarck heaved a deep sad sigh. This girl with the wheat-colored hair was unreal. She would vanish into oblivion as soon as Laoome lost interest in the world Markavvel. She was less than a shadow, less than a mirage, less than a dream. Lanarck looked over at Isabel, the Earth girl, who glared at him with sullen eyes. She was real enough.

They moved up the river and toward the white docks of Gahadion. Lanarck rose to his feet. He looked over the city, surveyed the folk on the dock who were clad in white, red and blue tunics, then turned to Jiro. "I'll have to take the weapon now."

"Stand back or I'll—" Lanarck took the weapon from her limp grasp. Isabel watched in sour amusement.

A dull throbbing sound, like the pulse of a tremendous heart, came down from the heavens. Lanarck cocked his head, listening. He scanned the sky. At the horizon appeared a strange cloud, like a band of white-gleaming metal, swelling in rhythm to the celestial throbbing. It lengthened with miraculous speed, until in all directions the horizon was encircled. The throb became a vast booming. The air itself seemed heavy, ominous. A terrible idea struck Lanarck. He turned and yelled to the awestruck oarsmen who were trailing their oars in the river.

"Quickly—get to the docks!"

They jerked at their oars, frantic, yet the galley moved no faster. The water of the river had become oily smooth, almost syrupy. The boat inched close to the dock. Lanarck was grimly aware of the terrified Isabel on one side of him, Jiro on the other.

"What is happening?" whispered Isabel. Lanarck watched the sky. The cloud-band of bright metal quivered and split into another which wobbled, bouncing just above.

"I hope I'm wrong," said Lanarck, "but I suspect that Laoome is going mad. Look at our shadows!" He turned to look at the sun, which jerked like a dying insect, vibrating through aimless arcs. His worst fears were realized.

"It can't be!" cried Isabel. "What will happen?"

"Nothing good."

The galley lurched against a pier. Lanarck helped Isabel and Jiro up to the dock, then followed.

Masses of tall golden-haired people milled in panic along the avenue.

"Lead me to the spaceboat!" Lanarck had to shout to

make himself heard over the tumult of the city. His mind
froze at a shocking thought: what would happen to Jiro?

He pushed the thought down. Isabel pulled at him urgently. "Come, hurry!"

Taking Jiro's hand, he ran off after Isabel toward the
black-porticoed temple at the far end of the avenue.

A constriction twisted the air; down came a rain of warm
red globules: small crimson jellyfish which stung naked flesh
like nettles. The din from the city reached hysterical pitch.
The red plasms increased to become a cloud of pink slime,
now oozing ankle-deep on the ground.

Isabel tripped and fell headlong in the perilous mess. She
struggled until Lanarck helped her to her feet.

They continued toward the temple, Lanarck supporting
both girls and keeping an uneasy eye on the structures to either side.

The rain of red things ceased, but the streets flowed with
ooze.

The sky shifted color—but what color? It had no place in
any spectrum. The color only a mad god could conceive.

The red slime curdled and fell apart like quicksilver, to jell
in an instant to millions upon millions of bright blue manikins three inches high. They ran, hopped, scuttled; the streets
were a quaking blue carpet of blank-faced little homunculi.
They clung to Lanarck's garments, they ran up his legs like
mice. He trod them under, heedless of their squeals.

The sun, jerking in small spasmodic motions, slowed, lost
its glare, became oblate. It developed striations and, as the
stricken population of Gahadion quieted in awe, the sun
changed to a segmented white slug, as long as five suns, as
wide as one. It writhed its head about and stared down
through the strange-colored sky at Markavvel.

In a delirium, the Gahadionites careened along the wide
avenues. Lanarck and the two girls almost were trod under as
they fought past a cross street.

In a small square, beside a marble fountain, the three
found refuge. Lanarck had reached a state of detachment: a
conviction that this experience was a nightmare.

A blue man-thing pulled itself into his hair. It was singing
in a small clear baritone. Lanarck set it upon the ground. His
mind grew calmer. This was no nightmare; this was reality,
however the word could be interpreted! Haste! The surge of
people had passed; the way was relatively open. "Let's go!"

He pulled at the two girls who had been watching the slug
which hung across the sky.

As they started off, there came the metamorphosis Lanarck
had been expecting, and dreading. The matter of Gahadion,
and all Markavvel, altered into unnatural substances. The
buildings of white marble became putty, slumped beneath
their own weight. The Malachite Temple, an airy dome on
green malachite pillars, sagged and slid to a sodden lump.
Lanarck urged the gasping girls to greater speed.

The Gahadionites no longer ran; there was no destination.
They stood staring up, frozen in horror by the glittering slug
in the sky. A voice screamed: "Laoome, Laoome!" Other
voices took up the cry: "Laoome, Laoome!"

If Laoome heard, he gave no sign.

Lanarck kept an anxious eye on these folk, dreading lest
they also, as dream-creatures, alter to shocking half-things.
For should they change, so would Jiro. Why take her to the
spaceboat? She could not exist outside the mind of
Laoome. . . . But how could he let her go?

The face of Markavvel was changing. Black pyramids
sprouted through the ground and, lengthening tremendously,
darted upward, to become black spikes, miles high.

Lanarck saw the spaceboat, still sound and whole, a product of more durable mind-stuff, perhaps, than Markavvel itself. Tremendous processes were transpiring beneath his feet,
as if the core of the planet itself were degenerating. Another
hundred yards to the spaceboat! "Faster!" he panted to the
girls.

All the while they ran, he watched the folk of Gahadion.
Like a cold wind blowing on his brain, he knew that the
change had come. He almost slowed his steps for despair.
The Gahadionites themselves knew. They staggered in unbe-
lieving surprise, regarding their hands, feeling their faces.

Too late! Unreasonably Lanarck had hoped that once in
space, away from Markavvel, Jiro might retain her identity.
But too late! A blight had befallen the Gahadionites. They
clawed their shriveling faces, tottered and fell, their shrunken
legs unable to support them.

In anguish Lanarck felt one of the hands he was holding
become hard and wrinkled. As her legs withered, he felt her
sag. He paused and turned, to look sadly upon what had been
Jiro.

The ground beneath his feet lurched. Around him twisted
dying Gahadionites. Above, dropping through the weird sky,

came the slug. Black spikes towered tremendously over his head. Lanarck heeded none of these. Before him stood Jiro—a Jiro gasping and reeling in exhaustion, but a Jiro sound and golden still! Dying on the marble pavement was the shriveled dream-thing he had known as Isabel May. Taking Jiro's hand, he turned and made for the spaceboat.

Hauling back the port, he pushed Jiro inside. Even as he touched the hull, he realized that the spaceboat was changing also. The cold metal had acquired a palpitant life of its own. Lanarck slammed shut the port, and, heedless of fracturing cold thrust-tubes, gushed power astern.

Off careened the spaceboat, dodging through the forest of glittering black spines, now hundreds of miles tall, swerving a thousand miles to escape the great slug falling inexorably to the surface of Markavvel. As the ship darted free into space, Lanarck looked back to see the slug sprawled across half a hemisphere. It writhed, impaled on the tall black spikes.

Lanarck drove the spaceboat at full speed toward the landmark star. Blue and luminous it shone, the only steadfast object in the heavens. All else poured in turbulent streams through black space: motes eddying in a pool of ink.

Lanarck looked briefly toward Jiro, and spoke. "Just when I decided that nothing else could surprise me, Isabel May died, while you, Jiro the Gahadionite, are alive."

"I am Isabel May. You knew already."

"I knew, yes, because it was the only possibility." He put his hand against the hull. The impersonal metallic feel had altered to a warm vitality. "Now, if we escape from this mess, it'll be a miracle."

Changes came quickly. The controls atrophied; the ports grew dull and opaque, like cartilage. Engines and fittings became voluted organs; the walls were pink moist flesh, pulsing regularly. From outside came a sound like the flapping of pinions; about their feet swirled dark liquid. Lanarck, pale, shook his head. Isabel pressed close to him.

"We're in the stomach of—something."

Isabel made no answer.

A sound like a cork popped from a bottle, a gush of gray light. Lanarck had guided the spaceboat aright; it had continued into the sane universe and its own destruction.

The two Earth creatures found themselves stumbling on the floor of Laoome's dwelling. At first they could not comprehend their deliverance; safety seemed but another shifting of scenes.

Lanarck regained his equilibrium. He helped Isabel to her feet; together they surveyed Laoome, who was still in the midst of his spasm. Rippling tremors ran along his black hide, the saucer eyes were blank and glazed.

"Let's go!" whispered Isabel.

Lanarck silently took her arm; they stepped out on the glaring wind-whipped plain. There, the two spaceboats, just as before. Lanarck guided Isabel to his craft, opened the port and motioned her inside. "I'm going back for one moment."

Lanarck locked the power-arm. "Just to guard against any new surprises."

Isabel said nothing.

Walking around to the spaceboat in which Isabel May had arrived, Lanarck similarly locked the mechanism. Then he crossed to the white concrete structure.

Isabel listened, but the moaning of the wind drowned out all other sounds. The chatter of a needle-beam? She could not be sure.

Lanarck emerged from the building. He climbed into the boat and slammed the port. They sat in silence as the thrust-tubes warmed, nor did they speak as he threw over the power-arm and the boat slanted off into the sky.

Not until they were far off in space did either of them speak.

Lanarck looked toward Isabel. "How did you know of Laoome?"

"Through my father. Twenty years ago he did Laoome some trifling favor—killed a lizard which had been annoying Laoome, or something of the sort."

"And that's why Laoome shielded you from me by creating the dream Isabel?"

"Yes. He told me you were coming down looking for me. He arranged that you should meet a purported Isabel May, that I might assess you without your knowledge."

"Why don't you look more like the photograph?"

"I was furious; I'd been crying; I was practically gnashing my teeth. I certainly hope I don't look like that."

"How about your hair?"

"It's bleached."

"Did the other Isabel know your identity?"

"I don't think so. No, I know she didn't. Laoome equipped her with my brain and all its memories. She actually was I."

Lanarck nodded. Here was the source of the inklings of recognition. He said thoughtfully: "She was very perceptive.

She said that you and I were, well, attracted to each other. I wonder if she was right."

"I wonder."

"There will be time to consider the subject. . . . One last point: the documents, with the over-ride."

Isabel laughed cheerfully. "There aren't any documents."

"No documents?"

"None. Do you care to search me?"

"Where are the documents?"

"Document, in the singular. A slip of paper. I tore it up."

"What was on the paper?"

"The over-ride. I'm the only person alive who knows it. Don't you think I should keep the secret to myself?"

Lanarck reflected a moment. "I'd like to know. That kind of knowledge is always useful."

"Where is the hundred million dollars you promised me?"

"It's back on Earth. When we get there you can use the over-ride."

Isabel laughed. "You're a most practical man. What happened to Laoome?"

"Laoome is dead."

"How?"

"I destroyed him. I thought of what we just went through. His dream-creatures—were they real? They seemed real to me, and to themselves. Is a person responsible for what happens during a nightmare? I don't know. I obeyed my instincts, or conscience, whatever it's called, and killed him."

Isabel May took his hand. "My instincts tell me that I can trust you. The over-ride is a couplet:

> "Tom, Tom, the piper's son
> Stole a pig and away he run."

# 5

Lanarck reported to Cardale. "I am happy to inform you that the affair is satisfactorily concluded."

Cardale regarded him skeptically. "What do you mean by that?"

"The over-ride is safe."

"Indeed? Safe where?"

"I thought it best to consult with you before carrying the over-ride on my person."

"That is perhaps over-discreet. What of Isabel May? Is she in custody?"

"In order to get the over-ride I had to make broad but reasonable concessions, including a full pardon, retraction of all charges against her, and official apologies as well as retributive payments for false arrest and general damages. She wants an official document, certifying these concessions. If you will prepare the document, I will transmit it, and the affair will be terminated."

Cardale said in a cool voice: "Who authorized you to make such far-reaching concessions?"

Lanarck spoke indifferently. "Do you want the over-ride?"

"Of course."

"Then do as I suggest."

"You're even more arrogant than Detering led me to expect."

"The results speak for themselves, sir."

"How do I know that she won't use the over-ride?"

"You can now call it up and change it, so I'm given to understand."

"How do I know that she hasn't used it already, to the hilt?"

"I mentioned compensatory payments. The adjustment has been made."

Cardale ran his fingers through his hair. "How much damages?"

"The amount is of no great consequence. If Isabel May had chosen to make intemperate demands, they would only partially balance the damage she has suffered."

"So you say." Cardale could not decide whether to bluster, to threaten, or to throw his hands in the air. At last he leaned back in his chair. "I'll have the document ready tomorrow, and you can bring in the over-ride."

"Very well, Mr. Cardale."

"I'd still like to know, unofficially, if you like, just how much she took in settlement."

"We requisitioned a hundred and one million, seven hundred and sixty-two dollars into a set of personal accounts."

Cardale stared. "I thought you said that she'd made a temperate settlement!"

"It seemed as easy to ask for a large sum as a small."

"No doubt even easier. It's a strange figure. Why seven hundred and sixty-two dollars?"

"That, sir, is money owing to me for which the bursar refuses to issue a voucher. It represents expenses in a previous case: bribes, liquor and the services of a prostitute, if you want the details."

"And why the million extra?"

"That represents a contingency fund for my own convenience, so that I won't be harassed in the future. In a quiet and modest sense it also reflects my annoyance with the bursar."

Lanarck rose to his feet. "I'll see you tomorrow at the same time, sir."

"Until tomorrow, Lanarck."

# Green Magic

Howard Fair, looking over the relics of his great uncle
Gerald McIntyre, found a large ledger entitled:

### WORKBOOK & JOURNAL
### Open at Peril!

Fair read the journal with interest, although his own work
went far beyond ideas treated only gingerly by Gerald
McIntyre.

"The existence of disciplines concentric to the elementary
magics must now be admitted without further controversy,"
wrote McIntyre. "Guided by a set of analogies from the
white and black magics (to be detailed in due course), I have
delineated the basic extension of purple magic, as well as its
corollary, Dynamic Nomism."

Fair read on, remarking the careful charts, the projections
and expansions, the transpolations and transformations by
which Gerald McIntyre had conceived his systemology. So
swiftly had the technical arts advanced that McIntyre's ex-
positions, highly controversial sixty years before, now seemed
pedantic and overly rigorous.

"Whereas benign creatures: angels, white sprites, merri-
hews, sandestins—are typical of the white cycle; whereas
demons, magners, trolls and warlocks are evinced by black
magic; so do the purple and green cycles sponsor their own
particulars, but these are neither good nor evil, bearing,
rather, the same relation to the black and white provinces
that these latter do to our own basic realm."

Fair reread the passage. The "green cycle"? Had Gerald
McIntyre wandered into regions overlooked by modern work-
ers?

He reviewed the journal in the light of this suspicion, and
discovered additional hints and references. Especially provoc-
ative was a bit of scribbled marginalia: "More concerning my

latest researches I may not state, having been promised an infinite reward for this forbearance."

The passage was dated a day before Gerald McIntyre's death, which had occurred on March 21, 1898, the first day of spring. McIntyre had enjoyed very little of his "infinite reward," whatever had been its nature. . . . Fair returned to a consideration of the journal, which, in a sentence or two, had opened a chink on an entire new panorama. McIntyre provided no further illumination, and Fair set out to make a fuller investigation.

His first steps were routine. He performed two divinations, searched the standard indexes, concordances, handbooks and formularies, evoked a demon whom he had previously found knowledgeable: all without success. He found no direct reference to cycles beyond the purple; the demon refused even to speculate.

Fair was by no means discouraged; if anything, the intensity of his interest increased. He reread the journal, with particular care to the justification for purple magic, reasoning that McIntyre, groping for a lore beyond the purple, might well have used the methods which had yielded results before. Applying stains and ultraviolet light to the pages, Fair made legible a number of notes McIntyre had jotted down, then erased.

Fair was immensely stimulated. The notes assured him that he was on the right track, and further indicated a number of blind alleys which Fair profited by avoiding. He applied himself so successfully that before the week was out he had evoked a sprite of the green cycle.

It appeared in the semblance of a man with green glass eyes and a thatch of young eucalyptus leaves in the place of hair. It greeted Fair with cool courtesy, would not seat itself, and ignored Fair's proffer of coffee.

After wandering around the apartment inspecting Fair's books and curios with an air of negligent amusement, it agreed to respond to Fair's questions.

Fair asked permission to use his tape-recorder, which the sprite allowed, and Fair set the apparatus in motion. (When subsequently he replayed the interview, no sound could be heard.)

"What realms of magic lie beyond the green?" asked Fair.

"I can't give you an exact answer," replied the sprite, "because I don't know. There are at least two more, corresponding to the colors we call rawn and pallow, and very likely others."

Fair arranged the microphone where it would more directly intercept the voice of the sprite.

"What," he asked, "is the green cycle like? What is its physical semblance?"

The sprite paused to consider. Glistening mother-of-pearl films wandered across its face, reflecting the tinge of its thoughts. "I'm rather severely restricted by your use of the word 'physical.' And 'semblance' involves a subjective interpretation, which changes with the rise and fall of the seconds."

"By all means," Fair said hastily, "describe it in your own words."

"Well—we have four different regions, two of which floresce from the basic skeleton of the universe, and so subsede the others. The first of these is compressed and isthiated, but is notable for its wide pools of mottle which we use sometimes for deranging stations. We've transplanted club-mosses from Earth's Devonian and a few ice-fires from Perdition. They climb among the rods which we call devil-hair—" he went on for several minutes but the meaning almost entirely escaped Fair. And it seemed as if the question by which he had hoped to break the ice might run away with the entire interview. He introduced another idea.

" 'Can we freely manipulate the physical extensions of Earth?' " The sprite seemed amused. "You refer, so I assume, to the various aspects of space, time, mass, energy, life, thought and recollections."

"Exactly."

The sprite raised its green corn-silk eyebrows. "I might as sensibly ask can you break an egg by striking it with a club? The response is on a similar level of seriousness."

Fair had expected a certain amount of condescension and impatience, and was not abashed. "How may I learn these techniques?"

"In the usual manner: through diligent study."

"Ah, indeed—but where could I study? Who would teach me?"

The sprite made an easy gesture, and whorls of green smoke trailed from his fingers to spin through the air. "I could arrange the matter, but since I bear you no particular animosity, I'll do nothing of the sort. And now, I must be gone."

"Where do you go?" Fair asked in wonder and longing. "May I go with you?"

The sprite, swirling a drape of bright green dust over its shoulders, shook his head. "You would be less than comfortable."

"Other men have explored the worlds of magic!"

"True: your uncle Gerald McIntyre, for instance."

"My uncle Gerald learned green magic?"

"To the limit of his capabilities. He found no pleasure in his learning. You would do well to profit by his experience and modify your ambitions." The sprite turned and walked away.

Fair watched it depart. The sprite receded in space and dimension, but never reached the wall of Fair's room. At a distance which might have been fifty yards, the sprite glanced back, as if to make sure that Fair was not following, then stepped off at another angle and disappeared.

Fair's first impulse was to take heed and limit his explorations. He was an adept in white magic, and had mastered the black art—occasionally he evoked a demon to liven a social gathering which otherwise threatened to become dull—but he had by no means illuminated every mystery of purple magic, which is the realm of Incarnate Symbols.

Howard Fair might have turned away from the green cycle except for three factors.

First was his physical appearance. He stood rather under medium height, with a swarthy face, sparse black hair, a gnarled nose, a small heavy mouth. He felt no great sensitivity about his appearance, but realized that it might be improved. In his mind's eye he pictured the personified ideal of himself: he was taller by six inches, his nose thin and keen, his skin cleared of its muddy undertone. A striking figure, but still recognizable as Howard Fair. He wanted the love of women, but he wanted it without the interposition of his craft. Many times he had brought beautiful girls to his bed, lips wet and eyes shining; but purple magic had seduced them rather than Howard Fair, and he took limited satisfaction in such conquests.

Here was the first factor which drew Howard Fair back to the green lore; the second was his yearning for extended, perhaps eternal, life; the third was simple thirst for knowledge.

The fact of Gerald McIntyre's death, or dissolution, or disappearance—whatever had happened to him—was naturally a matter of concern. If he had won to a goal so precious, why had he died so quickly? Was the "infinite reward" so miraculous, so exquisite, that the mind failed under its possession? (If such was the case, the reward was hardly a reward.)

Fair could not restrain himself, and by degrees returned to a study of green magic. Rather than again invoke the sprite whose air of indulgent contempt he had found exasperating, he decided to seek knowledge by an indirect method, employing the most advanced concepts of technical and cabalistic science.

He obtained a portable television transmitter which he loaded into his panel truck along with a receiver. On a Monday night in early May, he drove to an abandoned graveyard far out in the wooded hills, and there, by the light of a waning moon, he buried the television camera in graveyard clay until only the lens protruded from the soil.

With a sharp alder twig he scratched on the ground a monstrous outline. The television lens served for one eye, a beer bottle pushed neck-first into the soil the other.

During the middle hours, while the moon died behind wisps of pale cloud, he carved a word on the dark forehead; then recited the activating incantation.

The ground rumbled and moaned, the golem heaved up to blot out the stars.

The glass eyes stared down at Fair, secure in his pentagon.

"Speak!" called out Fair. *"Enteresthes, Akmai Adonai Bidemgir! Elohim, pa rahulli! Enteresthes, HVOI!* Speak!"

"Return me to earth, return my clay to the quiet clay from whence you roused me."

"First you must serve."

The golem stumbled forward to crush Fair, but was halted by the pang of protective magic.

"Serve you I will, if serve you I must."

Fair stepped boldly forth from the pentagon, strung forty yards of green ribbon down the road in the shape of a narrow V. "Go forth into the realm of green magic," he told the monster. "The ribbons reach forty miles, walk to the end, turn about, return, and then fall back, return to the earth from which you rose."

The golem turned, shuffled into the V of green ribbon, shaking off clods of mold, jarring the ground with its ponderous tread.

Fair watched the squat shape dwindle, recede, yet never reach the angle of the magic V. He returned to his panel truck, tuned the television receiver to the golem's eye, and surveyed the fantastic vistas of the green realm.

Two elementals of the green realm met on a spun-silver landscape. They were Jaadian and Misthemar, and they fell to discussing the earthen monster which had stalked forty miles through the region known as Cil; which then, turning in its tracks, had retraced its steps, gradually increasing its pace until at the end it moved in a shambling rush, leaving a trail of clods on the fragile moth-wing mosaics.

"Events, events, events," Misthemar fretted, "they crowd the chute of time till the bounds bulge. Or then again, the course is as lean and spare as a stretched tendon . . . But in regard to this incursion . . ." He paused for a period of reflection, and silver clouds moved over his head and under his feet.

Jaadian remarked, "You are aware that I conversed with Howard Fair; he is so obsessed to escape the squalor of his world that he acts with recklessness."

"The man Gerald McIntyre was his uncle," mused Misthemar. "McIntyre besought, we yielded; as perhaps now we must yield to Howard Fair."

Jaadian uneasily opened his hand, shook off a spray of emerald fire. "Events press, both in and out. I find myself unable to act in this regard."

"I likewise do not care to be the agent of tragedy."

A Meaning came fluttering up from below: "A disturbance among the spiral towers! A caterpillar of glass and metal has come clanking; it has thrust electric eyes into the Portinone and broke open the Egg of Innocence. Howard Fair is the fault."

Jaadian and Misthemar consulted each other with wry disinclination. "Very well, both of us will go; such a duty needs two souls in support."

They impinged upon Earth and found Howard Fair in a wall booth at a cocktail bar. He looked up at the two strangers and one of them asked, "May we join you?"

Fair examined the two men. Both wore conservative suits and carried cashmere topcoats over their arms. Fair noticed that the left thumb-nail of each man glistened green.

Fair rose politely to his feet. "Will you sit down?"

The green sprites hung up their overcoats and slid into the booth. Fair looked from one to the other. He addressed

Jaadian. "Aren't you he whom I interviewed several weeks ago?"

Jaadian assented. "You have not accepted my advice."

Fair shrugged. "You asked me to remain ignorant, to accept my stupidity and ineptitude."

"And why should you not?" asked Jaadian gently. "You are a primitive in a primitive realm; nevertheless not one man in a thousand can match your achievements."

Fair agreed, smiling faintly. "But knowledge creates a craving for further knowledge. Where is the harm in knowledge?"

Mithemar, the more mercurial of the sprites, spoke angrily. "Where is the harm? Consider your earthen monster! It befouled forty miles of delicacy, the record of ten million years. Consider your caterpillar! It trampled our pillars of carved milk, our dreaming towers, damaged the nerve-skeins which extrude and waft us our Meanings."

"I'm dreadfully sorry," said Fair. "I meant no destruction."

The sprites nodded. "But your apology conveys no guarantee of restraint."

Fair toyed with his glass. A waiter approached the table, addressed the two sprites. "Something for you two gentlemen?"

Jaadian ordered a glass of charged water, as did Misthemar. Fair called for another highball.

"What do you hope to gain from this activity?" inquired Misthemar. "Destructive forays teach you nothing!"

Fair agreed. "I have learned little. But I have seen miraculous sights. I am more than ever anxious to learn."

The green sprites glumly watched the bubbles rising in their glasses. Jaadian at last drew a deep sigh. "Perhaps we can obviate toil on your part and disturbance on ours. Explicitly, what gains or advantages do you hope to derive from green magic?"

Fair, smiling, leaned back into the red imitation-leather cushions. "I want many things. Extended life—mobility in time—comprehensive memory—augmented perception, with vision across the whole spectrum. I want physical charm and magnetism, the semblance of youth, muscular endurance . . . Then there are qualities more or less speculative, such as—"

Jaadian interrupted. "These qualities and characteristics we will confer upon you. In return you will undertake never again to disturb the green realm. You will evade centuries of toil; we will be spared the nuisance of your presence, and the inevitable tragedy."

"Tragedy?" inquired Fair in wonder. "Why tragedy?"

Jaadian spoke in a deep reverberating voice. "You are a man of Earth. Your goals are not our goals. Green magic makes you aware of our goals."

Fair thoughtfully sipped his highball. "I can't see that this is a disadvantage. I am willing to submit to the discipline of instruction. Surely a knowledge of green magic will not change me into a different entity?"

"No. And this is the basic tragedy!"

Misthemar spoke in exasperation. "We are forbidden to harm lesser creatures, and so you are fortunate; for to dissolve you into air would end all the annoyance."

Fair laughed. "I apologize again for making such a nuisance of myself. But surely you understand how important this is to me?"

Jaadian asked hopefully, "Then you agree to our offer?"

Fair shook his head. "How could I live, forever young, capable of extended learning, but limited to knowledge which I already see bounds to? I would be bored, restless, miserable."

"That well may be," said Jaadian. "But not so bored, restless and miserable as if you were learned in green magic."

Fair drew himself erect. "I must learn green magic. It is an opportunity which only a person both torpid and stupid could refuse."

Jaadian sighed. "In your place I would make the same response." The sprites rose to their feet. "Come then, we will teach you."

"Don't say we didn't warn you," said Misthemar.

Time passed. Sunset waned and twilight darkened. A man walked up the stairs, entered Howard Fair's apartment. He was tall, unobtrusively muscular. His face was sensitive, keen, humorous; his left thumb-nail glistened green.

Time is a function of vital processes. The people of Earth had perceived the motion of their clocks. On this understanding, two hours had elapsed since Howard Fair had followed the green sprites from the bar.

Howard Fair had perceived other criteria. For him the interval had been seven hundred years, during which he had lived in the green realm, learning to the utmost capacity of his brain.

He had occupied two years training his senses to the new

conditions. Gradually he learned to walk in the six basic three-dimensional directions, and accustomed himself to the fourth-dimensional short-cuts. By easy stages the blinds over his eyes were removed, so that the dazzling over-human intricacy of the landscape never completely confounded him.

Another year was spent training him to the use of a code language—an intermediate step between the vocalizations of Earth and the meaning patterns of the green realm, where a hundred symbol-flakes (each a flitting spot of delicate iridescence) might be displayed in a single swirl of import. During this time Howard Fair's eyes and brain were altered, to allow him the use of the many new colors, without which the meaning-flakes could not be recognized.

These were preliminary steps. For forty years he studied the flakes, of which there were almost a million. Another forty years was given to elementary permutations and shifts, and another forty to parallels, attenuation, diminishments and extensions; and during this time he was introduced to flake patterns, and certain of the more obvious displays.

Now he was able to study without recourse to the code language, and his progress becasme more marked. Another twenty years found him able to recognize more complicated Meanings, and he was introduced to a more varied program. He floated over the field of moth-wing mosaics, which still showed the footprints of the golem. He sweated in embarrassment, the extent of his wicked willfulness now clear to him.

So passed the years. Howard Fair learned as much green magic as his brain could encompass.

He explored much of the green realm, finding so much beauty that he feared his brain might burst. He tasted, he heard, he felt, he sensed, and each one of his senses was a hundred times more discriminating than before. Nourishment came in a thousand different forms: from pink eggs which burst into a hot sweet gas, suffusing his entire body; from passing through a rain of stinging metal crystals; from simple contemplation of the proper symbol.

Homesickness for Earth waxed and waned. Sometimes it was insupportable and he was ready to forsake all he had learned and abandon his hopes for the future. At other times the magnificence of the green realm permeated him, and the thought of departure seemed like the threat of death itself.

By stages so gradual he never realized them he learned green magic.

But the new faculty gave him no pride: between his crude

ineptitudes and the poetic elegance of the sprites remained a tremendous gap—and he felt his innate inferiority much more keenly than he ever had in his old state. Worse, his most earnest efforts failed to improve his technique, and sometimes, observing the singing joy of an improvised manifestation by one of the sprites, and contrasting it to his own labored constructions, he felt futility and shame.

The longer he remained in the green realm, the stronger grew the sense of his own maladroitness, and he began to long for the easy environment of Earth, where each of his acts would not shout aloud of vulgarity and crassness. At times he would watch the sprites (in the gossamer forms natural to them) at play among the pearl-petals, or twining like quick flashes of music through the forest of pink spirals. The contrast between their verve and his brutish fumbling could not be borne and he would turn away. His self-respect dwindled with each passing hour, and instead of pride in his learning, he felt a sullen ache for what he was not and could never become. The first few hundred years he worked with the enthusiasm of ignorance, for the next few he was buoyed by hope. During the last part of his time, only dogged obstinacy kept him plodding through what now he knew for infantile exercises.

In one terrible bittersweet spasm, he gave up. He found Jaadian weaving tinkling fragments of various magics into a warp of shining long splines. With grave courtesy, Jaadian gave Fair his attention, and Fair laboriously set forth his meaning.

Jaadian returned a message. "I recognize your discomfort, and extend my sympathy. It is best that you now return to your native home."

He put aside his weaving and conveyed Fair down through the requisite vortices. Along the way they passed Misthemar. No flicker of meaning was expressed or exchanged, but Howard Fair thought to feel a tinge of faintly malicious amusement.

Howard Fair sat in his apartment. His perceptions, augmented and sharpened by his sojourn in the green realm, took note of the surroundings. Only two hours before, by the clocks of Earth, he had found them both restful and stimulating; now they were neither. His books: superstition, spuriousness, earnest nonsense. His private journals and workbooks: a pathetic scrawl of infantilisms. Gravity tugged

at his feet, held him rigid. The shoddy construction of the
house, which heretofore he never had noticed, oppressed him.
Everywhere he looked he saw slipshod disorder, primitive
filth. The thought of the food he must now eat revolted him.

He went out on his little balcony which overlooked the
street. The air was impregnated with organic smells. Across
the street he could look into windows where his fellow hu-
mans lived in stupid squalor.

Fair smiled sadly. He had tried to prepare himself for
these reactions, but now was surprised by their intensity. He
returned into his apartment. He must accustom himself to the
old environment. And after all there were compensations.
The most desirable commodities of the world were now his to
enjoy.

Howard Fair plunged into the enjoyment of these
pleasures. He forced himself to drink quantities of expensive
wines, brandies, liqueurs, even though they offended his
palate. Hunger overcame his nausea, he forced himself to the
consumption of what he thought of as fried animal tissue, the
hypertrophied sexual organs of plants. He experimented with
erotic sensations, but found that beautiful women no longer
seemed different from the plain ones, and that he could
barely steel himself to the untidy contacts. He bought li-
braries of erudite books, glanced through them with contempt. He tried to amuse himself with his old magics; they
seemed ridiculous.

He forced himself to enjoy these pleasures for a month;
then he fled the city and established a crystal bubble on a
crag in the Andes. To nourish himself, he contrived a thick
liquid, which, while by no means as exhilarating as the substances of the green realm, was innocent of organic contami-
nation.

After a certain degree of improvisation and make-shift, he
arranged his life to its minimum discomfort. The view was
one of austere grandeur; not even the condors came to disturb him. He sat back to ponder the chain of events which
had started with his discovery of Gerald McIntyre's work-
book. He frowned. Gerald McIntyre? He jumped to his feet,
looked far over the crags.

He found Gerald McIntyre at a wayside service station in
the heart of the South Dakota prairie. McIntyre was sitting in
an old wooden chair, tilted back against the peeling yellow

paint of the service station, a straw hat shading his eyes from the sun.

He was a magnetically handsome man, blond of hair, brown of skin, with blue eyes whose gaze stung like the touch of icicle. His left thumbnail glistened green.

Fair greeted him casually; the two men surveyed each other with wry curiosity.

"I see you have adapted yourself," said Howard Fair.

McIntyre shrugged. "As well as possible. I try to maintain a balance between solitude and the pressure of humanity." He looked into the bright blue sky where crows flapped and called. "For many years I lived in isolation. I began to detest the sound of my own breathing."

Along the highway came a glittering automobile, rococo as a hybrid goldfish. With the perceptions now available to them, Fair and McIntyre could see the driver to be red-faced and truculent, his companion a peevish woman in expensive clothes.

"There are other advantages to residence here," said McIntyre. "For instance, I am able to enrich the lives of passersby with trifles of novel adventure." He made a small gesture; two dozen crows swooped down and flew beside the automobile. They settled on the fenders, strutted back and forth along the hood, fouled the windshield.

The automobile squealed to a halt, the driver jumped out, put the birds to flight. He threw an ineffectual rock, waved his arms in outrage, returned to his car, proceeded.

"A paltry affair," said McIntyre with a sigh. "The truth of the matter is that I am bored." He pursed his mouth and blew forth three bright puffs of smoke: first red, then yellow, then blazing blue. "I have arrived at the estate of foolishness, as you can see."

Fair surveyed his great-uncle with a trace of uneasiness. McIntyre laughed. "No more pranks. I predict, however, that you will presently share my malaise."

"I share it already," said Fair. "Sometimes I wish I could abandon all my magic and return to my former innocence."

"I have toyed with the idea," McIntyre replied thoughtfully. "In fact I have made all the necessary arrangements. It is really a simple matter." He led Fair to a small room behind the station. Although the door was open, the interior showed a thick darkness.

McIntyre, standing well back, surveyed the darkness with a quizzical curl to his lip. "You need only enter. All your magic, all your recollections of the green realm will depart. You will be no wiser than the next man you meet. And with your knowledge will go your boredom, your melancholy, your dissatisfaction."

Fair contemplated the dark doorway. A single step would resolve his discomfort.

He glanced at McIntyre; the two surveyed each other with sardonic amusement. They returned to the front of the building.

"Sometimes I stand by the door and look into the darkness," said McIntyre. "Then I am reminded how dearly I cherish my boredom, and what a precious commodity is so much misery."

Fair made himself ready for departure. "I thank you for this new wisdom, which a hundred more years in the green realm would not have taught me. And now—for a time, at least—I go back to my crag in the Andes."

McIntyre tilted his chair against the wall of the service station. "And I—for a time, at least—will wait for the next passerby."

"Good-bye, then, Uncle Gerald."

"Good-bye, Howard."

# The Ten Books

They were as alone as it is possible for living man to be in the black gulf between the stars. Far astern shone the suns of the home worlds—ahead the outer stars and galaxies in a fainter ghostly glimmer.

The cabin was quiet. Betty Welstead sat watching her husband at the assay table, her emotions tuned to his. When the centrifuge scale indicated heavy metal and Welstead leaned forward she leaned forward too in unconscious sympathy. When he burnt scrapings in the spectroscope and read *Lead* from the brightest pattern and chewed at his lips Betty released her pent-up breath, fell back in her seat.

Ralph Welstead stood up, a man of medium height—rugged, tough-looking—with hair and skin and eyes the same tawny color. He brushed the whole clutter of rock and ore into the waste chute and Betty followed him with her eyes.

Welstead said sourly, "We'd be millionaires if that asteroid had been inside the Solar system. Out here, unless it's pure platinum or uranium, it's not worth mining."

Betty broached a subject which for two months had been on the top of her mind. "Perhaps we should start to swing back in."

Welstead frowned, stepped up into the observation dome. Betty watched after him anxiously. She understood very well that the instinct of the explorer as much as the quest for minerals had brought them out so far.

Welstead stepped back down into the cabin. "There's a star ahead"—he put a finger into the three-dimensional chart—"this one right here, Eridanus two thousand nine hundred and thirty-two. Let's make a quick check—and then we'll head back in."

Betty nodded, suddenly happy. "Suits me." She jumped up, and together they went to the screen. He aimed the catch-all vortex, dialed the hurrying blur to stability and the star pulsed out like a white-hot coin. A single planet made up the entourage.

"Looks about Earth-size," said Welstead, interest in his voice, and Betty's heart sank a trifle. He tuned the circuit finer, turned up the magnification and the planet leapt at them.

"Look at that atmosphere! *Thick!*"

He swiveled across the jointed arm holding the thermocouple and together they bent over the dial.

"Nineteen degrees Centigrade. About Earth-norm. Let's look at that atmosphere. You know, dear, we might have something tremendous here! Earth-size, Earth temperature . . ." His voice fell off in a mutter as he peered through the spectroscope, flipping screen after screen past the pattern from the planet. He stood up, cast Betty a swift exultant glance, then squinted in sudden reflection. "Better make sure before we get too excited."

Betty felt no excitement. She watched without words as Welstead thumbed through the catalogue.

"*Whee!*" yelled Welstead, suddenly a small boy. "No listing! It's ours!" And Betty's heart melted at the news. Delay, months of delay, while Welstead explored the planet, charted its oceans and continents, classified its life. At the same time, a spark of her husband's enthusiasm caught fire in her brain and interest began to edge aside her gloom.

"We'll name it 'Welstead,'" he said. "Or, no—'Elizabeth' for you. A planet of your own! Some day there'll be cities and millions of people. And every time they write a letter or throw a shovelful of dirt or a ship lands—they'll use your name."

"No, dear," she said. "Don't be ridiculous. We'll call it 'Welstead'—for us both."

They felt an involuntary pang of disappointment later on when they found the planet already inhabited, and by men.

Yet their reception astonished them as much as the basic discovery of the planet and its people. Curiosity, hostility might have been expected. . . .

They had been in no hurry to land, preferring to fall into an orbit just above the atmosphere, the better to study the planet and its inhabitants.

It looked to be a cheerful world. There were a thousand kinds of forest, jungle, savannah. Sunny rivers coursed green fields. A thousand lakes and three oceans glowed blue. To the far north and far south snowfields glittered, dazzled. Such cit-

ies as they found—the world seemed sparsely settled—
merged indistinguishably with the countryside.

They were wide low cities, very different from the clanging
hives of Earth, and lay under the greenery like carvings in
alabaster or miraculous snowflakes. Betty, in whose nature
ran a strong streak of the romantic, was entranced.

"They look like cities of Paradise—cities in a dream!"

Welstead said reflectively, "They're evidently not backward. See that cluster of long gray buildings off to the side?
Those are factories."

Betty voiced a doubt which had been gradually forming
into words. "Do you think they might—resent our landing? If
they've gone to the trouble of creating a secret—well, call it
Utopia—they might not want to be discovered."

Welstead turned his head, gazed at her eye to eye. "Do you
want to land?" he asked soberly.

"Why, yes—if you do. If you don't think it's dangerous."

"I don't know whether it's dangerous or not. A people as
enlightened as those cities would seem to indicate would
hardly maltreat strangers."

Betty searched the face of the planet. "I think it would be
safe."

Welstead laughed. "I'm game. We've got to die sometime.
Why not out here?"

He jumped up to the controls, nosed the ship down.

"We'll land right in their laps, right in the middle of that
big city down there."

Betty looked at him questioningly.

"No sense sneaking down out in the wilds," said Welstead.
"If we're landing we'll land with a flourish."

"And if they shoot us for our insolence?"

"Call it Fate."

They bellied down into a park in the very center of the
city. From the observation dome Welstead glimpsed hurrying
knots of people.

"Go to the port, Betty. Open it just a crack and show yourself. I'll stay at the controls. One false move, one dead cat
heaved at us, and we'll be back in space so fast they won't
remember we arrived."

Thousands of men and women of all ages had surrounded
the ship, all shouting, all agitated by strong emotion.

"They're throwing flowers!" Betty gasped. She opened the
port and stood in the doorway and the people below shouted,
chanted, wept. Feeling rather ridiculous, Betty waved, smiled.

She turned to look back up at Welstead. "I don't know what we've done to deserve all this but we're heroes. Maybe they think we're somebody else."

Welstead craned his neck through the observation dome. "They look healthy—normal."

"They're beautiful," said Betty. "All of them."

The throng opened, a small group of elderly men and women approached. The leader, a white-haired man, tall, lean, with much the same face as Michelangelo's Jehovah, stood forth.

"Welcome!" he called resonantly. "Welcome from the people of Haven!"

Betty stared, and Welstead clambered down from the controls. The words were strangely pronounced, the grammar was archaic—but it was the language of Earth.

The white-haired man spoke on, without calculation, as if delivering a speech of great familiarity. "We have waited two hundred and seventy-one years for your coming, for the deliverance you will bring us."

Deliverance? Welstead considered the word. "Don't see much to deliver 'em from," he muttered aside to Betty. "The sun's shining, they look well-fed—a lot more enthusiastic than I do. Deliver 'em from what?"

Betty was climbing down to the ground and Welstead followed.

"Thanks for the welcome," said Welstead, trying not to sound like a visiting politician. "We're glad to be here. It's a wonderful experience, coming unexpectedly on a world like this."

The white-haired man bowed gravely. "Naturally you must be curious—as curious as we are about the civilized universe. But for the present, just one question for the ears of our world. How goes it with Earth?"

Welstead rubbed his chin, acutely conscious of the thousands of eyes, the utter silence.

"Earth," he said, "goes about as usual. There's the same seasons, the same rain, sunshine, frost and wind." And the people of Haven breathed in his words as devoutly as if they were the purest poetry. "Earth is still the center of the Cluster and there's more people living on Earth than ever before. More noise, more nuisance . . ."

"Wars? New governments? How far does science reach?"

Welstead considered. "Wars? None to speak of—not since

the Hieratic League broke up. The government still governs, uses lots of statistical machinery. There's still graft, robbery, inefficiency, if that's what you mean.

"Science—that's a big subject. We know a lot but we don't know a lot more, the way it's always been. Everything considered, it's the same Earth it's always been—some good, a lot of bad."

He paused, and the pent breath of the listeners went in a great sigh. The white-haired man nodded again, serious, sober—though evidently infected with the excitement that fired his fellows.

"No more for the present! You'll be tired and there's much time for talk. May I offer you the hospitality of my house?"

Welstead looked uncertainly at Betty. Instinct urged him not to leave his ship.

"Or if you'd prefer to remain aboard . . ." suggested the man of Haven.

"No," said Welstead. "We'll be delighted." If harm were intended—as emphatically did not seem likely—their presence aboard the ship would not prevent it. He craned his neck, looked here and there for the officialdom that would be bumptiously present on Earth.

"Is there anyone we should report to? Any law we'll be breaking by parking our ship here?"

The white-haired man laughed. "What a question! I am Alexander Clay, Mayor of this city Mytilene and Guide of Haven. By my authority and by common will you are free of anything the planet can offer you. Your ship will not be molested."

He led them to a wide low car and Betty was uncomfortably conscious of her blue shorts, rumpled and untidy by comparison with the many-colored tunics of the women in the crowd.

Welstead was interested in the car as providing a gauge of Haven's technics. Built of shiny gray metal it hung a foot above the ground, without the intervention of wheels. He gave Clay a startled look. "Anti-gravity? Your fortune's made."

Clay shook his head indulgently. "Magnetic fields, antipathetic to the metal in the road. Is it not a commonplace on Earth?"

"No," said Welstead. "The theory, of course, is well-known but there is too much opposition, too many roads to dig up. We still use wheels."

Clay said reflectively, "The force of tradition. The continuity which generates the culture of races. The stream we have been so long lost from. . . ."

Welstead shot him a sidelong glance. Clay was entirely serious.

The car had been sliding down the road at rather high speed through vistas of wonderful quiet and beauty. Every direction showed a new and separate enchantment—a glade surrounded by great trees, a small home of natural wood, a cluster of public buildings around a plaza, a terrace checkered with trees and lined with many-colored shops.

Occasionally there were touches of drama, such as the pylon at the end of a wide avenue. It rose two hundred feet into the air, a structure of concrete, bronze and black metal, and it bore the heroic figure of a man grasping vainly for a star.

Welstead craned his neck like a tourist. "Magnificent!"

Clay assented without enthusiasm. "I suppose it's not discreditable. Of course, to you, fresh from the worlds of civilization—" He left the sentence unfinished. "Excuse me, while I call my home." He bent his head to a telephone.

Betty said in Welstead's ear, "This is a city every planner on Earth would sell his soul to build."

Welstead grunted. "Remember Halleck?" he muttered. "He was a city planner. He wanted to tear down a square mile of slums in Lanchester, eighteen stories high on the average, nothing but airless three-room apartments.

"First the real estate lobby tore into him, called him a Chaoticist. A rumor circulated among his friends that he was morally degenerate. The poor devils that lived there tried to lynch him because they'd be evicted. The Old Faithfuls read him out of the party because they pulled the votes of the district. The slums are still there and Halleck's selling farm implements on Arcturus Five."

Betty looked off through the trees. "Maybe Haven will turn out to be an object lesson for the rest of the cluster."

Welstead shrugged. "Maybe, maybe not. Peace and seclusion are not something you can show to a million people— because it isn't peace and seclusion anymore."

Betty sat up straighter in her seat. "The only way to convince the unbelievers is by showing them, setting them an example. Do you think that if the Lanchester slum-dwellers saw this city they'd go back to their three-room apartments without wanting to do something about it?"

"If they saw this city," said Welstead, "they'd never leave Haven. By hook or crook, stowaway or workaway, they'd emigrate."

"Include me in the first wave!" said Betty indignantly.

The car turned into a leafy tunnel, crossed a carpet of bright green turf, stopped by a house built of dark massive wood. Four high gables in a row overlooked a terrace, where a stream followed its natural bed. The house looked spacious, comfortable—rather like the best country villas of Earth and the garden planets without the sense of contrived effect, the strain, the staging.

"My home," said Clay. He slid back a door of waxed blond wood, ushered them into an entry carpeted with golden rattan, walled with a fabric the color of the forest outside. A bench of glowing dark wood crossed a wall under a framed painting. From no apparent source light flooded the room, like water in a tank.

"One moment," said Clay with a trace of embarrassment. "My home is poor and makeshift enough without exposing it to your eyes at its worst." He was clearly sincere; this was no conventional deprecation.

He started away, paused and said to his half-comprehending guests, "I must apologize for our backwardness but we have no facilities for housing notable guests, no great inns or embassies or state-houses such as must add to the dignity of life on Earth. I can only offer you the hospitality of my home."

Welstead and Betty both protested. "We don't deserve as much. After all we're only a pair of fly-by-night prospectors."

Clay smiled and they could see that he had been put more at his ease. "You're the link between Haven and civilization—the most important visitors we've ever had. Excuse me." He departed.

Betty went to the picture on the wall, a simple landscape—the slope of a hill, a few trees, a distant range of mountains. Welstead, with small artistic sensibility, looked around for the source of the light—without success. He joined Betty beside the picture. She said half-breathlessly, "This is a—I'm afraid to say it—a masterpiece."

Welstead squinted, trying to understand the basis of his wife's awe and wonderment. Indeed the picture focused his eyes, drew them in and around the frame, infused him with a pleasant exhilaration, a warmth and serenity.

Clay, returning, noticed their interest. "What do you think of it?" he asked.

"I think it's—exceedingly well done," said Betty, at a loss for words which would convey her admiration without sounding fulsome.

Clay shook his head ruefully, turned away. "You need not praise an inconsequentiality out of courtesy, Mrs. Welstead. We know our deficiencies. Your eyes have seen the Giottos, the Rembrandts, the Cezannes. This must seem a poor thing."

Betty began to remonstrate but halted. Words evidently would not convince Clay—or perhaps a convention of his society prompted him to belittle the works of his people and it might be discourteous to argue too vehemently.

"Your quarters are being prepared," Clay told them. "I've also ordered fresh clothing for you both as I see yours are stained with travel."

Betty blushed, smoothed the legs of her blue shorts. Welstead sheepishly brushed at his faded blouse. He reached in his pocket, pulled out a bit of gravel. "From an asteroid I prospected a few weeks ago." He twisted it around in his fingers. "Nothing but granite, with garnet inclusions."

Clay took the bit of rock, inspected it with a peculiar reverence. "May I keep this?"

"Why, of course."

Clay laid the bit of stone on a silver plate. "You will not understand what this small stone symbolizes to us of Haven. Interstellar travel—our goal, our dream for two hundred and seventy-one years."

The recurrence of the period two hundred and seventy-one years! Welstead calculated. That put them back into the Era of the Great Excursives, when the over-under space-drive had first come into use, when men drove pell-mell through the galaxy, like bees through a field of flowers and human culture flared through space like a super-nova.

Clay led them through a large room, simple in effect, rich in detail. Welstead's vision was not analytical enough to catch every particular at first. He sensed overall tones of tan, brown, mellow blue, watery green, in the wood, fabric, glass, pottery—the colors combined to marvelous effect with the waxy umber gleam of natural wood. At the end of the room a case held ten large books bound in black leather and these, by some indefinable emphasis, seemed to bear the significance of an icon.

They passed through a passage open along one side into a

garden filled with flowers, low trees, tame birds. Clay showed them into a long apartment streaming with sunlight.

"Your bath is through the door," said Clay. "Fresh clothes are laid out on the bed. When you are rested I shall be in the main hall. Please be at leisure—the house is yours."

They were alone. Betty sighed happily, sank down on the bed. "Isn't it wonderful, dear?"

"It's queer," said Welstead, standing in the middle of the room.

"What's queer?"

"Mainly why these people, apparently gifted and efficient, act so humble, so self-deprecating."

"They look confident."

"They *are* confident. Yet as soon as the word Earth is mentioned it's like saying Alakland to an exiled Lak. There's nothing like it."

Betty shrugged, began to remove her clothes. "There's probably some very simple explanation. Right now I'm tired of speculating. I'm for that bath. Water, water, water! *Tons* of it!"

They found Clay in the long hall with his pleasant-faced wife, his four youngest children, whom he gravely introduced.

Welstead and Betty seated themselves on a divan and Clay poured them small china cups of pale yellow-green wine, then settled back in his own seat.

"First I'll explain our world of Haven to you—or have you surmised our plight?"

Welstead said, "I guess a colony was planted here and forgotten—lost."

Clay smiled sadly. "Our beginnings were rather more dramatic. Two hundred and seventy-one years ago the passenger packed *Etruria*, enroute to Rigel, went out of control. According to the story handed down to us the bus-bars fused inside the drive-box. If the case were opened the fields would collapse. If it were not the ship would fly until there was no more energy."

Welstead said, "That was a common accident in the old days. Usually the engineer cut away the thrust-blocks on one side of the hull. Then the ship flew in circles until help arrived."

Clay made a wry sad grimace. "No one on the *Etruria* thought of that. The ship left the known universe and finally passed close to a plane that seemed capable of sustaining life.

The sixty-three aboard took to the life-boats and so landed on Haven.

"Thirty-four men, twenty-five women, four children—ranging in age from Dorothy Pell, eight, to Vladimir Hocha, seventy-four, with representatives of every human race. We're the descendants of the sixty-three—three hundred million of us."

"Fast work," said Betty, with admiration.

"Large families," returned Clay. "I have nine children, sixteen grandchildren. From the start our guiding principle has been to keep the culture of Earth intact for our descendants, to teach them what we knew of human tradition.

"So that when rescue came—as it must finally—then our children or our children's children could return to Earth, not as savages but as citizens. And our invaluable source has been the Ten Books, the only books brought down from the *Etruria*. We could not have been favored with books more inspiring. . . ."

Clay's gaze went to the black bound books at the end of the room, and his voice lowered a trifle.

"The *Encyclopedia of Human Achievement*. The original edition was in ten little plastrol volumes, none of them larger than your hand—but in them was such a treasury of human glory that never could we forget our ancestry, or rest in our efforts to achieve somewhere near the level of the great masters. All the works of the human race we set as our standards—music, art, literature—all were described in the *Encyclopedia*."

"Described, you say," mused Welstead.

"There were no illustrations?" asked Betty.

"No," said Clay, "there was small compass for pictures in the original edition. However"—he went to the case, selected a volume at random—"the words left little to the imagination. For example, on the music of Bach—'When Bach arrived on the scene the toccata was tentative, indecisive—a recreation, a *tour de force*, where the musician might display his virtuosity.

"'In Bach the toccata becomes a medium of the noblest plasticity. The theme he suggests by casual fingering of the keyboard, unrelated runs. Then comes a glorious burst into harmony—the original runs glow like prisms, assume stature, gradually topple together into a miraculous pyramid of sound.'

"And on Beethoven—'A God among men. His music is the

voice of the world, the pageant of all imagined splendor. The sounds he invokes are natural forces of the same order as sunsets, storms at sea, the view from mountain crags.'

"And on Leon Bismarck Beiderbecke—'His trumpet pours out such a torrent of ecstasy, such triumph, such overriding joys that the heart of man freezes in anguish at not being wholly part of it.'" Clay closed the book, replaced it. "Such is our heritage. We have tried to keep alive, however poorly, the stream of our original culture."

"I would say that you have succeeded," Welstead remarked dryly.

Betty sighed, a long slow suspiration.

Clay shook his head. "You can't judge until you've seen more of Haven. We're comfortable enough though our manner of living must seem unimpressive in comparison with the great cities, the magnificent palaces of Earth."

"No, not at all," said Betty but Clay made a polite gesture.

"Don't feel obliged to flatter us. As I've said, we're aware of our deficiencies. Our music for instance—it is pleasant, sometimes exciting, sometimes profound, but never does it reach the heights of poignancy that the Encyclopedia describes.

"Our art is technically good but we despair of emulating Seurat, who 'out-lumens light,' or Braque, 'the patterns of the mind in patterns of color on the patterns of life,' or Cezanne—'the planes which under the guise of natural objects march, merge, meet in accord with remorseless logic, which wheel around and impel the mind to admit the absolute justice of the composition.'"

Betty glanced at her husband, apprehensive lest he speak what she knew must be on his mind. To her relief he kept silent, squinting thoughtfully at Clay. For her part Betty resolved to maintain a noncommittal attitude.

"No," Clay said heavily, "we do the best we can, and in some fields we've naturally achieved more than in others. To begin with we had the benefit of all human experience in our memories. The paths were charted out for us—we knew the mistakes to avoid. We've never had wars or compulsion. We've never permitted unreined authority. Still we've tried to reward those who are willing to accept responsibility.

"Our criminals—very few now—are treated for mental disorder on the first and second offense, sterilized on the third, executed on the fourth—our basic law being cooperation and contribution to the society, though there is infinite latitude in how this contribution shall be made. We do not make society a juggernaut. A man may live as integrally or as singularly as he wishes so long as he complies with the basic law."

Clay paused, looking from Welstead to Betty. "Now do you understand our way of living?"

"More or less," said Welstead. "In the outline at least. You seem to have made a great deal of progress technically."

Clay considered. "From one aspect, yes. From another no. We had the lifeboat tools, we had the technical skills and most important we knew what we were trying to do. Our main goal naturally has been the conquest of space. We've gone up in rockets but they can take us nowhere save around the sun and back. Our scientists are close on the secret of the space-drive but certain practical difficulties are holding them up."

Welstead laughed. "Space-drive can never be discovered by rational effort. That's a philosophical question which has been threshed back and forth for hundreds of years. Reason—the abstract idea—is a function of ordinary time and space. The space-drive has no qualities in common with these ideas and for this reason human thought can never consciously solve the problem of the overdrive. Experiment, trial and error can do it. Thinking about it is useless."

"Hm," said Clay. "That's a new concept. But now your presence makes it beside the point, for you will be the link back to our homeland."

Betty could see words trembling on her husband's tongue. She clenched her hands, willed—willed—*willed*. Perhaps the effort had some effect because Welstead merely said, "We'll do anything we can to help."

All of Mytilene they visited and nearby Tiryns, Dicte and Ilium. They saw industrial centers, atomic power generators, farms, schools. They attended a session of the Council of Guides, both making brief speeches, and they spoke to the people of Haven by television. Every news organ on the planet carried their words.

They heard music from a green hillside, the orchestra playing from under tremendous smoke black trees. They saw the art of Haven in public galleries, in homes and in common use. They read some of the literature, studied the range of the planet's science, which was roughly equivalent to that of

Earth. And they marveled continually how so few people in so little time could accomplish so much.

They visited the laboratories, where three hundred scientists and engineers strove to force magnetic, gravitic and vortigial fields into the fusion that made star-to-star flight possible. And the scientists watched in breathless tension as Welstead inspected their apparatus.

He saw at a single glance the source of their difficulty. He had read of the same experiments on Earth three hundred years ago and of the fantastic accident that had led Roman-Forteski and Gladheim to enclose the generatrix in a dodecahedron of quartz. Only by such a freak—or by his information—would these scientists of Haven solve the mystery of space-drive.

And Welstead walked thoughtfully from the laboratory, with the disappointed glances of the technicians following him out. And Betty had glanced after him in wonder, and the rest of the day there had been a strain between them.

That night as they lay in the darkness, rigid, wakeful, each could feel the pressure of the other's thoughts. Betty finally broke the silence, in a voice so blunt that there was no mistaking her feeling.

"Ralph!"

"What?"

"Why did you act as you did in the laboratory?"

"Careful," muttered Welstead. "Maybe the room is wired for sound."

Betty laughed scornfully. "This isn't Earth. These people are trusting, honest. . . ."

It was Welstead's turn to laugh—a short cheerless laugh. "And that's the reason I'm ignorant when it comes to space-drive."

Betty stiffened. "What do you mean?"

"I mean that these people are too damn good to ruin."

Betty relaxed, sighed, spoke slowly, as if she knew she was in for a long pull. "How—'ruin'?"

Welstead snorted. "It's perfectly plain. You've been to their homes, you've read their poetry, listened to their music. . . ."

"Of course. These people live every second of their lives with—well, call it exaltation. A devotion to creation like nothing I've ever seen before."

Welstead said somberly, "They're living in the grandest illusion ever imagined and they're riding for an awful fall. They're like a man on a glorious wine drunk."

Betty stared through the dark. "Are you crazy?"

"They're living in exaltation now," said Welstead, "but what a bump when the bubble breaks!"

"But why should it break?" cried Betty. "Why can't—"

"Betty," said Welstead with a cold sardonic voice, "have you ever seen a public park on Earth after a holiday?"

Betty said hotly, "Yes—it's dreadful. Because the people of Earth have no feeling of community."

"Right," said Welstead. "And these people have. They're knit very tightly by a compulsion that made them achieve in two hundred-odd years what took seven thousand on Earth. They're all facing in the same direction, geared to the same drive. Once that drive is gone how do you expect they'll hold on to their standards?"

Betty was silent.

"Human beings," said Welstead dreamily, "are at their best when the going's toughest. They're either at their best or else they're nothing. The going's been tough here—these people have come through. Give them a cheap living, tourist money—then what?

"But that's not all. In fact it's only half the story. These people here," he stated with emphasis, "are living in a dream. They're the victims of the Ten Books. They take every word literally and they've worked their hearts out trying to come somewhere near what they expect the standards to be.

"Their own stuff doesn't do half the things to them that the Ten Books says good art ought to do. Whoever wrote those Ten Books must have been a copywriter for an advertising agency." Welstead laughed. "Shakespeare wrote good plays—sure, I concede it. But I've never seen 'fires flickering along the words, gusty winds rushing through the pages.'

"Sibelius I suppose was a great composer—I'm no expert on these things—but whoever listened and became 'part of Finland's ice, moss-smelling earth, hoarse-breathing forest,' the way the Ten Books said everyone did?"

Betty said, "He was merely trying to express vividly the essence of the artists and musicians."

Betty said, "He was merely trying to express vividly the essence of the artists and musicians."

"Nothing wrong in that," said Welstead. "On Earth we're conditioned to call everything in print a lie. At least we allow for several hundred percent overstatement. These people out here aren't immunized. They've taken every word at its face value. The Ten Books is their Bible. They're trying to equal accomplishments which never existed."

Betty raised herself up on an elbow, said in a voice of hushed triumph, "And they've *succeeded!* Ralph, they've *succeeded!* They've met the challenge, they've equaled or beaten anything Earth has ever produced! Ralph, I'm proud to belong to the same race."

"Same species," Welstead corrected dryly. "These people are a mixed race. They're all races."

"What's the difference?" Betty snapped. "You're just quibbling. You know what I mean well enough."

"We're on a sidetrack," said Welstead wearily. "The question is not the people of Haven and their accomplishments. Of course they're wonderful—*now.* But how do you think contact with Earth will affect them?

"Do you think they'll continue producing when the challenge is gone? When they find the Earth is a rookery—nagging, quarreling—full of mediocre hacks and cheap mischief? Where the artists draw nothing but nude women and the musicians make their living reeling out sound, sound, sound—any kind of sound—for television sound-track. Where are all their dreams then?

"Talk about disappointment, staleness! Mark my words, half the population would be suicides and the other half would turn to prostitution and cheating the tourists. It's a tough proposition. I say, leave them with their dreams. Let them think we're the worst sort of villains. I say, get off the planet, get back where we belong."

Betty said in a troubled voice, "Sooner or later somebody else will find them."

"Maybe—maybe not. We'll report the region barren—which it is except for Haven."

Betty said in a small voice, "Ralph, I couldn't do it. I couldn't violate their trust."

"Not even to keep them trusting?"

Betty said wildly, "Don't you think there'd be an equal deflation if we sneaked away and left them? We're the climax to their entire two hundred and seventy-one years. Think of the listlessness after we left!"

"They're working on their space-drive," said Welstead. "Chances are a million to one against their stumbling on it. They don't know that. They've got a flicker of a field and they think all they have to do is adjust the power feed, get better insulation. They don't have the Mardi Gras lamp that Gladheim snatched up when the lead tank melted."

"Ralph," said Betty, "your words are all very logical. Your arguments stay together—but they're not satisfying emotionally. I don't have the feeling of rightness."

"Pish," said Welstead. "Let's not go spiritual."

"And," said Betty softly, "let's not try to play God either." There was a long silence.

"Ralph?" said Betty.

"What?"

"Isn't there *some* way . . ."

"Some way to do what?"

"Why should it be *our* responsibility?"

"I don't know whose else it is. We're the instruments—"

"But it's *their* lives."

"Betty," said Welstead wearily, "here's one time we can't pass the buck. We're the people who in the last resort say yes or no. We're the only people that see on both sides of the fence. It's an awful decision to make—but I say no."

There was no more talking and after an unmeasured period they fell asleep.

Three nights later Welstead stopped Betty as she began to undress for bed. She gave him a dark wide-eyed stare.

"Throw whatever you're taking into a bag. We're leaving."

Betty's body was rigid and tense, slowly relaxing as she took a step toward him. "Ralph . . ."

"What?" And she could find no softness, no indecision in his topaz eyes.

"Ralph—it's *dangerous* for us to go. If they caught us, they'd execute us—for utter depravity." And she said in a murmur, looking away, "I suppose they'd be justified too."

"It's a chance we'll have to take. Just what we said the day we decided to land. We've got to die sometime. Get your gear and let's take off."

"We should leave a note, Ralph. Something . . ."

He pointed to an envelope. "There it is. Thanking them for their hospitality. I told them we were criminals and couldn't risk returning to Earth. It's thin but it's the best I could do."

A hint of fire returned to Betty's voice. "Don't worry, they'll believe it."

Sullenly she tucked a few trinkets into a pouch. "It's a long way to the ship you know," she warned him.

"We'll take Clay's car. I've watched him and I know how to drive it."

She jerked in a small bitter spasm of laughter. "We're even car thieves."

"Got to be," said Welstead stonily. He went to the door, listened. The utter silence of honest sleep held the rest of the house. He returned to where Betty stood waiting, watching him coldly with an air of dissociation.

"This way," said Welstead. "Out through the terrace."

They passed out into the moonless night of Haven and the only sound was the glassy tinkle of the little stream that ran in its natural bed through the terrace.

Welstead took Betty's hand. "Easy now, don't walk into that bamboo." He clutched and they froze to a halt. Through a window had come a sound—a gasp—and then the relieved mutter a person makes on waking from a bad dream.

Slowly, like glass melting under heat, the two came to life, stole across the terrace, out upon the turf beside the house. They circled the vegetable garden and the loom of the car bulked before them.

"Get in," whispered Welstead. "I'll push till we're down around the bend."

Betty climbed into the seat and her foot scraped against the metal. Welstead stiffened, listened, pierced the darkness like an eagle. Quiet from the house, the quiet of relaxation, of trust. . . . He pushed at the car and it floated easily across the ground, resisting his hand only through inertia.

It jerked to a sudden halt. And Welstead froze in his tracks again. A burglar alarm of some sort. No, there were no thieves on Haven—except two recently-landed people from Earth. A trap?

"The anchor," whispered Betty.

Of course—Welstead almost groaned with relief. Every car had an anchor to prevent the wind from blowing it away. He found it, hooked it into place on the car's frame and now the car floated without hindrance down the leafy tunnel that was Clay's driveway. Around a bend he ran to the door, jumped in, pressed his foot on the power pedal, and the car slid away with the easy grace of a canoe. Out on the main road he switched on the lights and they rushed off through the night.

"And we still use wheels on Earth," said Welstead. "If we only had a tenth of the guts these people have—"

Cars passed them from the other direction. The lights

glowed briefly into their faces and they cringed low behind
the windscreen.

They came to the park where their ship lay. "If anyone
stops us," Welstead said in Betty's ear, "we've just driven
down to get some personal effects. After all we're not prison-
ers."

But he circled the ship warily before stopping beside it and
then he waited a few seconds, straining his eyes through the
darkness. But there was no sound, no light, no sign of any
guard or human presence.

Welstead jumped from the car. "Fast now. Run over,
climb inside. I'll be right behind you."

They dashed through the dark, up the rungs welded to the
hull, and the cold steel felt like a caress to Welstead's hot
hands. Into the cabin; he thudded the port shut, slammed
home the dogs.

Welstead vaulted to the controls, powered the reactors.
Dangerous business—but once clear of the atmosphere they
could take time to let them warm properly. The ship rose; the
darkness and lights of Mytilene fell below. Welstead sighed,
suddenly tired, but warm and relaxed.

Up, up—and the planet became a ball, and Eridanus two
thousand nine hundred and thirty-two peered around the edge
and suddenly, without any noticeable sense of boundary
passed, they were out in space.

Welstead sighed. "Lord, what a relief! I never knew how
good empty space could look."

"It looks beautiful to me also," said Alexander Clay. "I've
never seen it before."

Welstead whirled, jumped to his feet.

Clay came forward from the reaction chamber, watching
with a peculiar expression Welstead took to be deadly fury.
Betty stood by the bulkhead, looking from one to the other,
her face blank as a mirror.

Welstead came slowly down from the controls. "Well—
you've caught us in the act. I suppose you think we're
treating you pretty rough. Maybe we are. But my conscience is
clear. And we're not going back. Looks like you asked for a
ride, and you're going to get one. If necessary—" He paused
meaningfully.

Then, "How'd you get aboard?" and after an instant of
narrow-eyed speculation, "And why? Why tonight?"

Clay shook his head slowly. "Ralph—you don't give us any
credit for ordinary intelligence, let alone ordinary courage."

"What do you mean?"

"I mean that I understand your motives—and I admire you for them. Although I think you've been bull-headed putting them into action without discussing it with the people most directly concerned."

Welstead lowered his head, stared with hard eyes. "It's basically my responsibility. I don't like it but I'm not afraid of it."

"It does you credit," said Clay mildly. "On Haven we're used to sharing responsibility. Not diluting it, you understand, but putting a dozen—a hundred—a thousand minds on a problem that might be too much for one. You don't appreciate us, Ralph. You think we're soft, spiritless."

"No," said Welstead. "Not exactly—"

"Our civilization is built on adaptability, on growth, on flexibility," continued Clay. "We—"

"You don't understand just what you'd have to adapt to," said Welstead harshly. "It's nothing nice. It's graft, scheming sharp-shooters, tourists by the million, who'll leave your planet the way a platoon of invading soldiers leaves the first pretty girl they find."

"There'll be problems," said Clay. His voice took on power. "But that's what we want, Ralph—problems. We're hungry for them, for the problems of ordinary human existence. We want to get back into the stream of life. And if it means grunting and sweating we want it. We're flesh and blood, just like you are.

"We don't want Nirvana—we want to test our strength. We want to fight along with the rest of decent humanity. Don't you fight what you think is unjust?"

Welstead slowly shook his head. "Not any more. It's too big for me. I tried when I was young, then I gave up. Maybe that's why Betty and I roam around the outer edges."

"No," said Betty. "That's not it at all, Ralph, and you know it. You explore because you like exploring. You like the rough and tumble of human contact just as much as anyone else."

"Rough and tumble," said Clay, savoring the words. "That's what we need on Haven. They had it in the old days. They gave themselves to it, beating the new world into submission. It's ours now. Another hundred years of nowhere to go and we'd be drugged, lethargic, decadent."

Welstead was silent.

"The thing to remember, Ralph," said Clay, "is that we're part of humanity. If there's good going, fine. But if there are problems we want to help lick them. You said you'd given up because it was too big for you. Do you think it would be too big for a whole planet? Three hundred million hard honest brains?"

Welstead stared, his imagination kindled. "I don't see how—"

Clay smiled. "I don't either. It's a problem for three hundred million minds. Thinking about it that way it doesn't seem so big. If it takes three hundred brains three days to figure out a dodecahedron of quartz—"

Welstead jerked, looked accusingly at his wife. "Betty!"

She shook her head. "I told Clay about our conversation, our argument. We discussed it all around. I told him everything—and I told him I'd give a signal whenever we started to leave. But I never mentioned spacedrive. If they discovered it they did it by themselves."

Welstead turned slowly back to Clay. "*Discovered* it? But—that's impossible."

Clay said, "Nothing's impossible. You yourself gave me the hint when you told me human reason was useless because the space-drive worked out of a different environment. So we concentrated not on the drive itself but on the environment. The first results came at us in terms of twelve directions— hence the dodecahedron. Just a hunch, an experiment and it worked."

Welstead sighed. "I'm licked. I give in. Clay, the headache is yours. You've *made* it yours. What do you want to do? Go back to Haven?"

Clay smiled, almost with affection. "We're this far. I'd like to see Earth. For a month, incognito. Then we'll come back to Haven and make a report to the world. And then there's three hundred million of us, waiting for the bell in round one."

# Chateau d'If

## CHAPTER I

### Roll of the Dice

The advertisement appeared on a telescreen commercial, and a few days later at the side of the news-fax. The copy was green on a black background, a modest rectangle among the oranges, reds, yellows. The punch was carried in the message:

Jaded? Bored?
Want ADVENTURE?
Try the Chateau d'If.

The Oxonian Terrace was a pleasant area of quiet in the heart of the city—a red-flagged rectangle dotted with beach umbrellas, tables, lazy people. A bank of magnolia trees screened off the street and filtered out most of the street noise; the leakage, a soft sound like surf, underlay the conversation and the irregular *thud-thud-thud* from the Oxonian handball courts.

Roland Mario sat in complete relaxation, half-slumped, head back, feet propped on the spun-air and glass table—in the same posture as his four companions. Watching them under half-closed lids, Mario pondered the ancient mystery of human personality. How could men be identical and yet each completely unique?

To his left sat Breaugh, a calculator repairman. He had a long bony nose, round eyes, heavy black eyebrows, a man deft with his fingers, methodical and patient. He had a Welsh name, and he looked the pure ancient Welsh type, the small dark men that had preceded Caesar, preceded the Celts.

Next to him sat Janniver. North Europe, Africa, the Orient

had combined to shape his brain and body. An accountant by trade, he was a tall spare man with short yellow hair. He had a long face with features that first had been carved, then kneaded back, blunted. He was cautious, thoughtful, a tough opponent on the handball court.

Zaer was the quick one, the youngest of the group. Fair-skinned with red cheeks, dark curly hair, eyes gay as valentines, he talked the most, laughed the most, occasionally lost his temper.

Beside him sat Ditmar, a sardonic man with keen narrow eyes, a high forehead, and a dark bronze skin from Polynesia, the Sudan, or India, or South America. He played no handball, consumed fewer highballs than the others, because of a liver disorder. He occupied a well-paying executive position with one of the television networks.

And Mario himself, how did they see him? He considered. Probably a different picture in each of their minds, although there were few pretensions or striking features to his exterior. He had nondescript pleasant features, hair and eyes without distinction, skin the average golden-brown. Medium height, medium weight, quiet-spoken, quietly dressed. He knew he was well-liked, so far as the word had meaning among the five; they had been thrown together not so much by congeniality as by the handball court and a common bachelorhood.

Mario became aware of the silence. He finished his high-ball. "Anyone go another round?"

Breaugh made a gesture of assent.

"I've got enough," said Janniver.

Zaer tilted the glass down his throat, set it down with a thud. "At the age of four I promised my father never to turn down a drink."

Ditmar hesitated, then said, "Might as well spend my money on liquor as anything else."

"That's all money is good for," said Breaugh. "To buy a little fun into your life."

"A lot of money buys a lot of fun," said Ditmar morosely. "Try and get the money."

Zaer gestured, a wide, fanciful sweep of the arm. "Be an artist, an inventor, create something, build something. There's no future working for wages."

"Look at this new crop of schoolboy wonders," said Breaugh sourly. "Where in the name of get-out do they come from? Spontaneous generation by the action of sunlight on slime? . . . All of a sudden, nothing but unsung geniuses, everywhere you look. De Satz, Coley—atomicians. Honn, Versovitch, Lekky, Brule, Richards—administrators. Gandelip, New, Cardosa—financiers. Dozens of them, none over twenty-three, twenty-four. All of 'em come up like meteors."

"Don't forget Pete Zaer," said Zaer. "He's another one, but he hasn't meteored yet. Give him another year."

"Well," muttered Ditmar, "maybe it's a good thing. Somebody's got to do our thinking for us. We're fed, we're clothed, we're educated, we work at soft jobs, and good liquor's cheap. That's all life means for ninety-nine out of a hundred."

"If they'd only take the hangover out of the liquor," sighed Zaer.

"Liquor's a release from living," said Janniver somberly. "Drunkenness is about the only adventure left. Drunkenness and death."

"Yes," said Breaugh. "You can always show contempt for life by dying."

Zaer laughed. "Whiskey or cyanide. Make mine whisky."

Fresh highballs appeared. They shook dice for the tag. Mario lost, signed the check.

After a moment Breaugh said, "It's true though. Drunkenness and death. The unpredictables. The only two places left to go—unless you can afford twenty million dollars for a planetary rocket. And even then there's only dead rock after you get there."

Ditmar said, "You overlooked a third possibility."

"What's that?"

"The Chateau d'If."

All sat quiet; then all five shifted in their chairs, settling back or straightening themselves.

"Just what is the Chateau d'If?" asked Mario.

"*Where* is it?" asked Zaer. "The advertisement said 'Try the Chateau d'If,' but it said nothing about how or where."

Janniver grunted. "Probably a new nightclub."

Mario shook his head doubtfully. "The advertisement gave a different impression."

"It's not a night club," said Ditmar. All eyes swung to him. "No, I don't know what it is. I know *where* it is, but only because there's been rumors a couple months now."

"What kind of rumors?"

"Oh—nothing definite. Just hints. To the effect that *if* you want adventure, *if* you've got money to pay for it, *if* you're willing to take a chance, *if* you have no responsibilities you can't abandon—"

"If—if—if," said Breaugh with a grin. "The Chateau d'If."

Ditmar nodded. "That's it exactly."

"Is it dangerous?" asked Zaer. "If all they do is string a tight-wire across a snake-pit, turn a tiger loose at you, and you can either walk tight-rope or fight tiger, I'd rather sit here and drink high-balls and figure how to beat Janniver in the tournament."

Ditmar shrugged. "I don't know."

Breaugh frowned. "It could be a dope-den, a new kind of bordello."

"There no such thing," said Zaer. "It's a haunted house with real ghosts."

"If we're going to include fantasy," said Ditmar, "a time machine."

"If," said Breaugh.

There was a short ruminative silence.

"It's rather peculiar," said Mario. "Ditmar says there've been rumors a couple months now. And last week an advertisement."

"What's peculiar about it?" asked Janniver. "That's the sequence in almost any new enterprise."

Breaugh said quickly, "That's the key word—'enterprise.' The Chateau d'If is not a natural phenomenon; it's a man-created object, idea, process—whatever it is. The motive behind it is a human motive—probably money."

"What else?" asked Zaer whimsically.

Breaugh raised his black eyebrows high. "Oh, you never know. Now, it can't be a criminal enterprise, otherwise the ACP would be swarming all over it."

Ditmar leaned back, swung Breaugh a half-mocking look. "The Agency of Crime Prevention can't move unless there's an offense, unless someone signs a complaint. If there's no overt offense, no complaint, the law can't move."

Breaugh made an impatient gesture. "Very true. But that's a side issue to the idea I was trying to develop."

Ditmar grinned. "Sorry. Go on."

"What are the motives which prompt men to new enterprises? First, money, which in a sense comprises, includes, all of the other motives too. But for the sake of clarity, call this first, the desire for money, an end in itself. Second, there's the will for power. Subdivide that last into, say, the crusading instinct and call it a desire for unlimited sexual opportunity.

Power over women. Then third, curiosity, the desire to know. Fourth, the enterprise for its own sake, as a diversion. Like a millionaire's race horses. Fifth, philanthropy. Any more?"

"Covers it," said Zaer.

"Possibly the urge for security, such as the Egyptian pyramids," suggested Janniver.

"I think that's the fundamental motive behind the first category, the lust for money."

"Artistic spirit, creativeness."

"Oh, far-fetched, I should say."

"Exhibitionism," Ditmar put forward.

"Equally far-fetched."

"I disagree. A theatrical performance is based solely and exclusively, from the standpoint of the actors, upon their mania for exhibitionism."

Breaugh shrugged. "You're probably right."

"Religious movements, missions."

"Lump that under the will to administer power."

"It sticks out at the edges."

"Not far. . . . That all? Good. What does it give us? Anything suggestive?"

"The Chateau d'If!" mused Janniver. "It still sounds like an unnecessarily florid money-making scheme."

"It's not philanthropy—at least superficially," said Mario. "But probably we could fabricate situations that would cover any of your cases."

Ditmar made an impatient gesture. "Talk's useless. What good is it? Not any of us know for sure. Suppose it's a plot to blow up the city?"

Breaugh said coolly, "I appoint you a committee of one, Ditmar, to investigate and report."

Ditmar laughed sourly. "I'd be glad to. But I've got a better idea. Let's roll the dice. Low man applies to the Chateau d'If—financed by the remaining four."

Breaugh nodded. "Suits me. I'll roll with you."

Ditmar looked around the table.

"What's it cost?" asked Zaer.

Ditmar shook his head. "I've no idea. Probably comes high."

Zaer frowned, moved uneasily in his seat. "Set a limit of two thousand dollars per capita."

"Good, so far as I'm concerned. Janniver?"

The tall man with the short yellow hair hesitated. "Yes, I'll roll. I've nothing to lose."

"Mario?"

"Suits me."

Ditmar took up the dice box, cupped it with his hand, rattled the dice. "The rules are for poker dice. One throw, ace high. In other words, a pair of aces beats a pair of sixes. Straight comes between three of a kind and a full house. That suit everybody? . . . Who wants to roll first?"

"Go ahead, shoot," said Mario mildly.

Ditmar shook, shook, shook, turned the dice out. Five bodies leaned forward, five pair of eyes followed the whirling cubes. They clattered down the table, clanged against a highball glass, came to rest.

"Looks like three fives," said Ditmar. "Well, that's medium good."

Mario, sitting on his left, picked up the box, tossed the dice in, shook, threw. He grunted. A two, a three, a four, a five, a four. "Pair of fours. Ouch."

Breaugh threw silently. "Three aces."

Janniver threw. "Two pair. Deuces and threes."

Zaer, a little pale, picked up the dice. He flashed a glance at Mario. "Pair of fours to beat." He shook the dice, shook—then threw with a sudden flourish. Clang, clatter among the glasses. Five pairs of eyes looked. Ace, deuce, three, six, deuce.

"Pair of deuces."

Zaer threw himself back with a tight grin. "Well, I'm game. I'll go. It's suppose to be an adventure. Of course they don't say whether you come out alive or not."

"You should be delighted," said Breaugh, stuffing tobacco in his pipe. "After all it's our money that's buying you this mysterious thrill."

Zaer made a helpless gesture with both hands. "Where do I go? What do I do?" He looked at Ditmar. "Where do I get this treatment?"

"I don't know," said Ditmar. "I'll ask at the studio. Somebody knows somebody who's been there. Tomorrow about this time I'll have the details, as much as I can pick up, at any rate."

Now came a moment of silence—a silence combined of several peculiar qualities. Each of the five contributed a component, but which the wariness, which the fear, which the quiet satisfaction, it was impossible to say.

Breaugh set down his glass. "Well, Zaer, what do you think? Ready for the tight-rope or the tiger?"

"Better take a pair of brass knuckles or a ring-flash," said Ditmar with a grin.

Zaer glanced around the circle of eyes, laughed ruefully. "The interest you take in me is flattering."

"We want a full report. We want you to come out alive."

Zaer said, "I want to come out alive too. Who's going to stake me to the smelling salts and adrenalin, in case the adventure gets really adventurous?"

"Oh, you look fit enough," said Breaugh. He rose to his feet. "I've got to feed my cats. There's the adventure in my life—taking care of seven cats. Quite a futile existence. The cast love it." He gave a sardonic snort. "We're living a life men have dreamed of living ever since they first dreamed. Food, leisure, freedom. We don't know when we're well off."

# CHAPTER II

## Changed Man

Zaer was scared. He held his arms tight against his body, and his grin, while wide and ready as ever, was a half-nervous grimace, twisted off to the side. He made no bones about his apprehension, and sat in his chair on the terrace like a prizefighter waiting for the gong.

Janniver watched him solemnly, drinking beer. "Maybe the *idea* of the Chateau d'If is adventure enough."

" 'What is adventure?' asked jesting Zaer, and did not stay for the answer," said Breaugh, eyes twinkling. He loaded his pipe.

"Adventure is just another name for having the daylights scared out of you and living to tell about it," said Zaer wretchedly.

Mario laughed. "If you never show up again, we'll know it wasn't a true adventure."

Breaugh craned his neck around. "Where's Ditmar? He's the man with all the information."

"Here he comes," said Zaer. "I feel like a prisoner."

"Oh, the devil!" said Breaugh. "You don't need to go through with it if you don't want to. After all, it's just a lark. No matter of life or death."

Zaer shook his head. "No, I'll try her on."

Ditmar pulled up a chair, punched the service button, ordered beer. Without preamble he said, "It costs eight thousand. It costs *you* eight thousand, that is. There's two levels.

Type A costs ten million; Type B, ten thousand, but they'll take eight. Needless to say, none of us can go two and a half million, so you're signed up on the Type B schedule."

Zaer grimaced. "Don't like the sound of it. It's like a fun house at the carnival. Some of 'em go through the bumps, others stand around watching, waiting for somebody's dress to blow up. And there's the lad who turns the valves, throws the switches. He has the real fun."

Ditmar said, "I've already paid the eight thousand, so you fellows can write me checks. We might as well get that part over now, while I've got you all within reach."

He tucked the checks from Mario, Janniver and Breaugh into his wallet. "Thanks." He turned to Zaer. "This evening at six o'clock, go to this address." He pushed a card across the table. "Give whoever answers the door this card."

Breaugh and Mario, on either side of Zaer, leaned over, scrutinized the card along with Zaer. It read:

THE CHATEAU D'IF
5600 Exmoor Avenue
Meadowlands

In the corner were scribbled the words: "Zaer, by Sutlow."

"I had to work like blazes to get it," said Ditmar. "It seems they're keeping it exclusive. I had to swear to all kinds of things about you. Now for heaven's sake, Zaer, don't turn out to be an ACP agent or I'm done with Sutlow, and he's my boss."

"ACP?" Zaer raised his eyebrows. "Is it—illegal?"

"I don't know," said Ditmar. "That's what I'm spending two thousand dollars on you for."

"I hope you have a damn good memory," said Breaugh with a cool grin. "Because—if you live—I want two thousand dollars' worth of vicarious adventure."

"If I die," retorted Zaer, "buy yourself a Ouija board; I'll still give you your money's worth."

"Now," said Ditmar, "we'll meet here Tuesdays and Fridays at three—right, fellows?"—he glanced around the faces—"until you show up."

Zaer rose. "Okay. Tuesdays and Fridays at three. Be seeing you." He waved a hand that took in them all, and stumbling slightly, walked away.

"Poor kid," said Breaugh. "He's scared stiff."

Tuesday passed. Friday passed. Another Tuesday, another Friday, and Tuesday came again. Mario, Ditmar, Breaugh, Janniver reached their table at three o'clock, and with subdued greetings, took their seats.

Five minutes, ten minutes passed. Conversation trickled to a halt. Janniver sat square to the table, big arms resting beside his beer, occasionally scratching at his short yellow hair, or rubbing his blunt nose. Breaugh, slouched back in the seat, looked sightlessly out through the passing crowds. Ditmar smoked passively, and Mario twirled and balanced a bit of paper he had rolled into a cylinder.

At three-fifteen Janniver cleared his throat. "I guess he went crazy."

Breaugh grunted. Ditmar smiled a trifle. Mario lit a cigarette, scowled.

Janniver said, "I saw him today."

Six eyes swung to him. "Where?"

"I wasn't going to mention it," said Janniver, "unless he failed to show up today. He's living at the Atlantic-Empire— a suite on the twentieth floor. I bribed the clerk and found that he's been there over a week."

Breaugh said with a wrinkled forehead, eyes black and suspicious, "How did you happen to see him there?"

"I went to check their books. It's on my route. On my way out, I saw Zaer in the lobby, big as life."

"Did he see you?"

Janniver shrugged woodenly. "Possibly. I'm not sure. He seemed rather wrapped up in a woman, an expensive-looking woman."

"Humph," said Ditmar. "Looks like Zaer's got our money's worth, all right."

Breaugh rose. "Let's go call on him, find out why he hasn't been to see us." He turned to Janniver. "Is he registered under his own name?"

Janniver nodded his long heavy head. "As big as life."

Breaugh started away, halted, looked from face to face. "You fellows coming?"

"Yes," said Mario. He rose. So did Ditmar and Janniver.

The Atlantic-Empire Hotel was massive and elegant, equipped with every known device for the feeding, bathing, comforting, amusing, flattering, relaxing, stimulating, assuaging of the men and women able to afford the price.

At the entry a white-coated flunky took the wraps of the most casual visitor, brushed him, offered the woman corsages from an iced case. The hall into the lobby was as hushed as the nave of a cathedral, lined with thirtyfoot mirrors. A moving carpet took the guest into the lobby, a great hall in the Gloriana style of fifty years before. An arcade of small shops lined one wall. Here—if the guest cared little for expense—he could buy wrought copper, gold, tantalum; gowns in glowing fabrics of scarlet, purple, indigo; *objets* from ancient Tibet and the products of Novacraft; cabochons of green Jovian opals, sold by the milligram, blue balticons from Mars, fire diamonds brought from twenty miles under the surface of the Earth; Marathesti cherries preserved in Organdy Liqueur, perfumes pressed from Arctic moss, white marmorea blooms like the ghosts of beautiful women.

Another entire wall was a single glass panel, the side of the hotel's main swimming pool. Underwater shone blue-green, and there was the splash, the shining wet gold of swimming bodies. The furniture of the lobby was in shades of the same blue-green and gold, with intimacy provided by screens of vines covered with red, black and white blossoms. A golden light suffused the air, heightened the illusion of an enchanted world where people moved in a high-keyed *milieu* of expensive clothes, fabulous jewelry, elegant wit, careful lovemaking.

Breaugh looked about with a twisted mouth. "Horrible parasites, posing and twittering and debauching each other while the rest of the world works!"

"Oh, come now," said Ditmar. "Don't be so all-fired intense. They're the only ones left who are having any fun."

"I doubt it," said Breaugh. "They're as defeated and futile as anyone else. There's no more place for them to go than there is for us."

"Have you heard of the Empyrean Tower?"

"Oh—vaguely. Some tremendous building out in Meadowlands."

"That's right. A tower three miles high. Somebody's having fun with that project. Designing it, seeing it go up, up, up."

"There's four billion people in the world," said Breaugh. "Only one Empyrean Tower."

"What kind of a world would it be without extremes?" asked Ditmar. "A place like the inside of a filing cabinet. Breathe the air here. It's rich, smells of civilization, tradition."

Mario glanced in surprise at Ditmar, the saturnine wry Ditmar, whom he would have considered the first to sneer at the foibles of the elite.

Janniver said mildly, "I enjoy coming here, myself. In a way, it's an adventure, a look into a different world."

Breaugh snorted. "Only a millionaire can do anything more than look."

"The mass standard of living rises continuously," reflected Mario. "And almost at the same rate the number of millionaires drops. Whether we like it or not, the extremes are coming closer together. In fact, they've almost met."

"And life daily becomes more like a bowl of rich, nourishing mush—without salt," said Ditmar. "By all means abolish poverty, but let's keep our millionaires. . . . Oh, well, we came here to find Zaer, not to argue sociology. I suppose we might as well all go together."

They crossed the lobby. The desk clerk, a handsome silver-haired man with a grave face, bowed.

"Is Mr. Zaer in?" Ditmar asked.

"I'll call his suite, sir." A moment later: "No, sir, he doesn't answer. Shall I page him?"

"No," said Ditmar. "We'll look around a bit."

"About an hour ago I believe he crossed the lobby toward the Mauna Hiva. You might try there."

"Thanks."

The Mauna Hiva was a circular room. At its center rose a great mound of weathered rock, overgrown with palms, ferns, a tangle of exotic plants. Three coconut palms slanted across the island, and the whole was lit with a soft watery white light. Below was a bar built of waxed tropical woods, and beyond, at the periphery of the illumination, a ring of tables.

They found Zaer quickly. He sat with a dark-haired woman in the sheath of emerald silk. On the table in front of them moved a number of small glowing many-colored shapes—sparkling, flashing, intense as patterns cut from butterfly wings. It was a ballet, projected in three-dimensional miniature. Tiny figures leaped, danced, posed to entrancing music in a magnificent setting of broken marble columns and Appian cypress trees.

After a moment the four stood back, watching in dour amusement.

Breaugh nudged Mario. "By heaven, he acts like he's been doing it all his life!"

Ditmar advanced to the table; the girl turned her long opaque eyes up at him. Zaer glanced up blankly.

"Hello there, Zaer," said Ditmar, a sarcastic smile wreath-

ing his lips. "Have you forgotten your old pals of the Oxonian Terrace?"

Zaer stared blankly. "I'm sorry."

"I suppose you don't know us?" asked Breaugh, looking
down his long crooked nose.

Zaer pushed a hand through his mop of curly black hair.
"I'm afraid you have the advantage of me, gentlemen."

"Humph," said Breaugh. "Let's get this straight. You're
Pete Zaer, are you not?"

"Yes, I am."

Janniver interposed, "Perhaps you'd prefer to speak with
us alone?"

Zaer blinked. "Not at all. Go ahead, say it."

"Ever heard of the Chateau d'If?" inquired Breaugh acidly.

"And eight thousand dollars?" added Ditmar. "A joint in-
vestment, shall we say?"

Zaer frowned in what Mario could have sworn to be honest bewilderment.

"You believe that I owe you eight thousand dollars?"

"Either that, or eight thousand dollars' worth of information."

Zaer shrugged. "Eight thousand dollars?" He reached into
his breast pocket, pulled out a bill-fold, counted. "One, two,
three, four, five, six, seven, eight. There you are, gentlemen.
Whatever it's for, I'm sure I don't know. Maybe I was
drunk." He handed eight thousand-dollar bills to the rigid
Ditmar. "Anyway now you're satisfied and I hope you'll be
good enough to leave." He gestured to the tiny figures, swaying, posturing, to the rapturous music. "We've already missed
the Devotional Dance, the main reason we tuned it on."

"Zaer," said Mario haltingly. The gay youthful eyes swung
to him.

"Yes?"—politely.

"Is this all the report we get? After all, we acted in good
faith."

Zaer stared back coldly. "You have eight thousand dollars. I don't know you from Adam's off ox. You claim it, I
pay it. That's pretty good faith on my part."

Breaugh pulled at Mario's arm. "Let's go."

# CHAPTER III

## *Blind Plunge*

Soberly they sat a table in an unpretentious tavern, drinking beer. For a while none of the four spoke. Four silent figures—tall strong Janniver, with the rough features, the Baltic hair, the African fiber, the Oriental restraint; Breaugh, the nimble-eyed, black browed and long-nosed; Ditmar, the sardonic autumn-colored man with the sick liver; Mario, normal, modest, pleasant.

Mario spoke first. "If that's what eight thousand buys at the Chateau d'If, I'll volunteer."

"If," said Breaugh shortly.

"It's not reasonable," rumbled Janniver. Among them, his emotions were probably the least disturbed, his sense of order and fitness the most outraged.

Breaugh struck the table with his fist, a light blow, but nevertheless vehement. "It's *not* reasonable! It violates logic!"

"*Your* logic," Ditmar pointed out.

Breaugh cocked his head sideways. "What's yours?"

"I haven't any."

"I maintain that the Chateau d'If is an *enterprise*," said Breaugh. "At the fee they charged, I figured it for a money-making scheme. It looks like I'm wrong. Zaer was broke a month ago. Or almost so. We gave him eight thousand dollars. He goes to the Chateau d'If, he comes out, takes a suite at the Atlantic-Empire, buys an expensive woman, shoves money at us by the fistful. The only place he could have got it is at the Chateau d'If. Now there's no profit in that kind of business."

"Some of them pay ten million dollars," said Mario softly. "That could take up some of the slack."

Ditmar drank his beer. "What now? Want to shake again?"

No one spoke. At last Breaugh said, "Frankly, I'm afraid to."

Mario raised his eyebrows. "What? With Zaer's climb to riches right in front of you?"

"Odd," mused Breaugh, "that's just what he was saying. That he was one of the meteoric schoolboy wonders who hadn't meteored yet. Now he'll probably turn out to be an unsung genius."

"The Chateau still sounds good, if that's what it does for you."

"If," sneered Breaugh.

"If," assented Mario mildly.

Ditmar said with a harsh chuckle, "I've got eight thousand dollars here. Our mutual property. As far as I'm concerned, it's all yours, if you want to take on Zaer's assignment."

Breaugh and Janniver gave acquiescent shrugs.

Mario toyed with the idea. His life was idle, useless. He dabbled in architecture, played handball, slept, ate. A pleasant but meaningless existence. He rose to his feet. "I'm on my way, right now. Give me the eight thousand before I change my mind."

"Here you are," said Ditmar. "Er—in spite of Zaer's example, we'll expect a report. Tuesdays and Fridays at three, on the Oxonian Terrace."

Mario waved gaily, as he pushed out the door into the late afternoon. "Tuesdays and Fridays at three. Be seeing you."

Ditmar shook his head. "I doubt it."

Breaugh compressed his mouth. "I doubt it too."

Janniver merely shook his head. . . .

Exmoor Avenue began in Lanchester, in front of the Power Bank, on the fourth level, swung north, rose briefly to the fifth level where it crossed the Continental Highway, curved back to the west, slanted under Grimshaw Boulevard, dropped to the surface in Meadowlands.

Mario found 5600 Exmoor to be a gray block of a building, not precisely dilapidated, but evidently unloved and uncared-for. A thin indecisive strip of lawn separated it from the road, and a walkway led to a small excrescence of a portico.

With the level afternoon sun shining full on his back, Mario walked to the portico, pressed the button.

A moment passed, then the door slid aside, revealing a short hall. "Please come in," said the soft voice of a commercial welcome-box.

Mario advanced down the hall, aware that radiation was scanning his body for metal or weapons. The hall opened into a green and brown reception room, furnished with a leather settee, a desk, a painting of three slim wide-eyed nudes against a background of a dark forest. A door flicked back, a young woman entered.

Mario tightened his mouth. It was an adventure to look at the girl. She was amazingly beautiful, with a beauty that grew more poignant the longer he considered it. She was silent, small-boned. Her eyes were cool, direct, her jaw and chin fine and firm. She was beautiful in herself, without ornament, ruse or adornment; beautiful almost in spite of herself, as if she regretted the magic of her face. Mario felt cool detachment in her gaze, an impersonal unfriendliness. Human perversity immediately aroused in his brain a desire to shatter the indifference, to arouse passion of one sort or another. . . . He smothered the impulse. He was here on business.

"Your name, please?" Her voice was soft, with a fine grain to it, like precious wood, and pitched in a strange key.

"Roland Mario."

She wrote on a form. "Age?"

"Twenty-nine."

"Occupation?"

"Architect."

"What do you want here?"

"This is the Chateau d'If?"

"Yes." She waited, expectantly.

"I'm a customer."

"Who sent you?"

"No one. I'm a friend of Pete Zaer's. He was here a couple of weeks ago."

She nodded, wrote.

"He seems to have done pretty well for himself," observed Mario cheerfully.

She said nothing until she had finished writing. Then: "This is a business, operated for profit. We are interested in money. How much do you have to spend?"

"I'd like to know what you have to sell."

"Adventure." She said the word without accent or emphasis.

"Ah," said Mario. "I see. . . . Out of curiosity, how does working here affect you? Do you find it an adventure, or are you bored too?"

She shot him a quick glance. "We offer two classes of service. The first we value at ten million dollars. It is cheap at that price, but it is the dullest and least stirring of the two—the situation over which you have some control. The second we value at ten thousand dollars, and this produces the most extreme emotions with the minimum of immediate control on your part."

Mario considered the word "immediate." He asked, "Have you been through the treatment?"

Again the cool flick of a glance. "Would you care to indicate how much you wish to spend?"

"I asked you a question," said Mario.

"You will receive further information inside."

"Are you human?" asked Mario. "Do you breathe?"

"Would you care to indicate how much you have to spend?"

Mario shrugged. "I have eight thousand dollars with me." He pursed his lips. "And I'll give you a thousand to stick your tongue out at me."

She dropped the form into a slot, arose. "Follow me, please."

She led him through the door, along a hall, into a small room, bare and stark, lit by a single cone-shaped floor lamp turned against the ceiling, a room painted white, gray, green. A man sat at a desk punching a calculator. Behind him stood a filing cabinet. There was a faint odor in the air, like mingled mint, gardenias, with a hint of an antiseptic, medicinal scent.

The man looked up, rose to his feet, bowed his head politely. He was young, blond as beach-sand, as magnificently handsome as the girl was beautiful. Mario felt a slight edge form in his brain. One at a time they were admirable, their beauty seemed natural. Together, the beauty cloyed, as if it were something owned and valued highly. It seemed self-conscious and vulgar. And Mario suddenly felt a quiet pride in his own commonplace person.

The man was taller than Mario by several inches. His chest was smooth and wide corded with powerful sinew. In spite of almost over-careful courtesy, he gave an impression of overpowering, overriding confidence.

"Mr. Roland Mario," said the girl. She added drily, "He's got eight thousand dollars."

The young man nodded gravely, reached out his hand. "My name is Mervyn Allen." He looked at the girl. "Is that all, Thane?"

"That's all for tonight." She left.

"Can't keep going on eight thousand a night," grumbled Mervyn Allen. "Sit down, Mr. Mario."

Mario took a seat. "The adventure business must have tremendous expenses," he observed with a tight grin.

"Oh, no," said Allen with wide candid eyes. "To the contrary. The operators have a tremendous avarice. We try to average twenty million a day profit. Occasionally we can't make it."

"Pardon me for annoying you with carfare," said Mario. "If you don't want it, I'll keep it."

Allen made a magnanimous gesture. "As you please."

Mario said, "The receptionist told me that ten million buys the dullest of your services, and ten thousand something fairly wild. What do I get for nothing? Vivisection?"

Allen smiled. "No. You're entirely safe with us. That is to say, you suffer no physical pain, you emerge alive."

"But you won't give me any particulars? After all, I have a fastidious nature. What you'd consider a good joke might annoy me very much."

Mervyn Allen shrugged blandly. "You haven't spent any money yet. You can still leave."

Mario rubbed the arms of his chair with the palms of his hand. "That's rather unfair. I'm interested, but also I'd like to know something of what I'm getting into."

Allen nodded. "Understandable. You're willing to take a chance, but you're not a complete fool. Is that it?"

"Exactly."

Allen straightened a pencil on his desk. "First, I'd like to give you a short psychiatric and medical examination. You understand," and he flashed Mario a bright candid glance, "we don't want any accidents at the Chateau d'If."

"Go ahead," said Mario.

Allen slid open the top of his desk, handed Mario a cap of crinkling plastic in which tiny wires glittered. "Encephalograph pick-up. Please fit it snugly."

Mario grinned. "Call it a lie-detector."

Allen smiled briefly. "A lie-detector, then."

Mario muttered, "I'd like to put it on you."

Allen ignored him, pulled out a pad of printed forms, adjusted a dial in front of him.

"Name?"

"Roland Mario."

"Age?"

"Twenty-eight."

Allen stared at the dial, frowned, looked up questioningly.

"I wanted to see if it worked," said Mario. "I'm twenty-nine."

"It works," said Allen shortly. "Occupation?"

"Architect. At least I dabble at it, design dog houses and rabbit hutches for my friends. Although I did the Geraf

Fleeter Corporation plant in Hanover a year or so ago, pretty big job."

"*Hm*. Where were you born?"

"Buenos Aires."

"Ever hold any government jobs? Civil Service? Police? Administrative? ACP?"

"No."

"Why not?"

"Red tape. Disgusting bureaucrats."

"Nearest relative?"

"My brother, Arthur Mario. In Callaco. Coffee business."

"No wife?"

"No wife."

"Approximate worth? Wealth, possessions, real estate?"

"Oh—sixty, seventy thousand. Modestly comfortable. Enough so that I can loaf all I care to."

"Why did you come to the Chateau d'If?"

"Same reason that everybody else comes. Boredom. Repressed energy. Lack of something to fight against."

Allen laughed. "So you think you'll work off some of that energy fighting the Chateau d'If?"

Mario smiled faintly. "It's a challenge."

"We've got a good thing here," Allen confided. "A wonder it hasn't been done before. How did you happen to come to the Chateau d'If?"

"Five of us rolled dice. A man named Pete Zaer lost. He came, but he wouldn't speak to us afterwards."

Allen nodded sagely. "We've got to ask that our customers keep our secrets. If there were no mystery, we would have no customers."

"It had better be good," said Mario, "after all the build-up." And he thought he saw a flicker of humor in Allen's eyes.

"It's cheap at ten million."

"And quite dear at ten thousand?" suggested Mario.

Allen leaned back in his chair, and his beautiful face was cold as a marble mask. Mario suddenly thought of the girl in the front office. The same expression of untouchable distance and height. He said, "I suppose you have the same argument with everyone who comes in."

"Identically."

"Well, where do we go from here?"

"Are you healthy? Any organic defects?"

"None."

"Very well. I'll waive the physical."

Mario reached up, removed the encephalograph pick-up. "Now I can lie again."

Allen drummed a moment on the tabletop, reached forward, tossed the mesh back in the desk, scribbled on a sheet of paper, tossed it to Mario. "A contract relieving us of responsibility."

Mario read. In consideration of services rendered, Roland Mario agreed that the Chateau d'If and its principals would not be held responsible for any injuries, physical or psychological, which he might sustain while on the premises, or as a result of his presence on the premises. Furthermore, he waived all rights to prosecute. Any and all transactions, treatments, experiments, events which occurred on, by or to his person were by his permission and express direction.

Mario chewed doubtfully at his lip. "This sounds pretty tough. About all you can't do is kill me."

"Correct," said Allen.

"A very ominous contract."

"Perhaps just the talk is adventure enough," suggested Allen, faintly contemptuous.

Mario pursed his lips. "I like pleasant adventures. A nightmare is an adventure, and I don't like nightmares."

"Who does?"

"In other words, you won't tell me a thing?"

"Not a thing."

"If I had any sense," said Mario, "I'd get up and walk out."

"Suit yourself."

"What do you do with all the money?"

Mervyn Allen relaxed in his chair, put his hands behind his blond head. "We're building the Empyrean Tower. That's no secret."

It was news to Mario. The Empyrean Tower—the vastest, grandest, heaviest, tallest, most noble structure created or even conceived by man. A sky-piercing star-aspiring shaft three miles tall.

"Why, if I may ask, are you building the Empyrean Tower?"

Allen sighed. "For the same reason you're here, at the Chateau d'If. Boredom. And don't tell me to take my own treatment."

"Have you?"

Allen studied him with narrow eyes. "Yes. I have. You ask lots of questions. Too many. Here's the contract. Sign it or tear it up. I can't give you any more time."

"First," said Mario patiently, "you'll have to give me some idea of what I'm getting into."

"It's not crime," said Allen. "Let's say—we give you a new outlook on life."

"Artificial amnesia?" asked Mario, remembering Zaer.

"No. Your memory is intact. Here it is," and Allen thrust out the contract. "Sign it or tear it up."

Mario signed. "I realize I'm a fool. Want my eight thousand?"

"We're in the business for money," said Allen shortly. "If you can spare it."

Mario counted out the eight thousand-dollar bills. "There you are."

Allen took the money, tapped it on the table, inspected Mario ruminatively. "Our customers fall pretty uniformly into three groups. Reckless young men just out of adolescence, jaded old men in search of new kinds of vice, and police snoopers. You don't seem to fit."

Mario said with a shrug. "Average the first two. I'm reckless, jaded and twenty-nine."

Allen smiled briefly, politely, rose to his feet. "This way, please."

A panel opened behind him, revealing a chamber lit with cool straw-colored light. Green plants, waist-high, grew in profusion—large-leafed exotics, fragile ferns, fantastic spired fungi, nodding spear-blades the color of Aztec jade. Mario noticed Allen drawing a deep breath before entering the room, but thought nothing of it. He followed, gazing right and left in admiration for the small artificial jungles to either side. The air was strong with the mint-gardenia-antiseptic odor—pungent. He blinked. His eyes watered, blurred. He halted, swaying. Allen turned around, watched with a cool half-smile, as if this were a spectacle he knew well but found constantly amusing.

Vision retreated; hearing hummed, flagged, departed; time swam, spun. . . .

# CHAPTER IV

## *A New Life*

Mario awoke.

It was a sharp clean-cut awakening, not the slow wading through a morass of drug.

He sat on a bench in Tanagra Square, under the big mimosa, and the copper peacocks were pecking at bread he held out to them.

He looked at his hand. It was a fat pudgy hand. The arm was encased in hard gray fiber. No suit he owned was gray. The arm was short. His legs were short. His belly was large. He licked his lips. They were pulpy, thick.

He was Roland Mario inside the brain, the body was somebody else. He sat quite still.

The peacocks pecked at the bread. He threw it away. His arm was stiff, strangely heavy. He had flabby muscles. He rose to his feet grunting. His body was soft but not flexible. He rubbed his hand over his face, felt a short lumpy nose, long ears, heavy cheeks like pans full of cold glue. He was bald as the underside of a fish.

Who was the body? He blinked, felt his mind twisting, tugging at its restraint. Mario fought to steady himself, as a man in a teetering canoe tries to hold it steady, to prevent capsizing into dark water. He leaned against the trunk of the mimosa tree. Steady, steady, focus your eyes! What had been done to him no doubt could be undone. Or it would wear off. Was it a dream, an intensely vivid segment of narcotiana? Adventure—ha! That was a mild word.

He fumbled into his pockets, found a folded sheet of paper. He opened it, sat down while he read the typescript. First there was a heavy warning:

MEMORIZE THE FOLLOWING, AS THIS PAPER WILL DISINTEGRATE IN APPROXIMATELY FIVE MINUTES!

You are embarking on the life you paid for.

Your name is Ralston Ebery. Your age is 56. You are married to Florence Ebery, age 50. Your home address is 19 Seafoam Place. You have three children: Luther, age 25, Ralston Jr., age 23, Clydia, age 19.

You are a wealthy manufacturer of aircraft, the

Ebery Air-car. Your bank is the African Federal;
the pass-book is in your pocket. When you sign
your name, do not consciously guide your hand; let
the involuntary muscles write the signature Ralston
Ebery.

If you dislike your present form, you may return
to the Chateau d'If. Ten thousand dollars will buy
you a body of your choice, ten million dollars will
buy you a young healthy body to your own specifi-
cations.

Please do not communicate with the police. In
the first place, they will believe you to be insane. In
the second place, if they successfully hampered the
operation of the Chateau d'If, you would be
marooned in the body of Ralston Ebery, a prospect
you may or may not enjoy. In the third place, the
body of Roland Mario will insist on his legal identity.

With your business opportunities, ten million dollars is a sum well within your reach. When you
have it return to the Chateau d'If for a young and
healthy body.

We have fulfilled our bargain with you. We have
given you adventure. With skill and ingenuity, you
will be able to join the group of men without age,
eternally young.

Mario read the sheet a second time. As he finished, it
crumbled into dust in his hands. He leaned back, aware of
nausea rising in him like an elevator in a shaft. The most
hateful of intimacies, dwelling in another man's body—especially one so gross and untidy. He felt a sensation of hunger, and with perverse malice decided to let Ralston Ebery's
body go hungry.

Ralston Ebery! The name was vaguely familiar. Did Ralston Ebery now possess Mario's own body? Possibly. Not
necessarily. Mario had no conception of the principle involved in the transfer. There seemed to be no incision, no
brain graft.

Now what?

He could report to the ACP. But, if he could make them
believe him, there still would be no legal recourse. To the
best of his knowledge, no one at the Chateau d'If had per-

formed a criminal act upon him. There was not even a good case of battery, since he had waived his right to prosecute.

The newspapers, the telescreens? Suppose unpleasant publicity were able to force the Chateau d'If out of business, what then? Mervyn Allen could set up a similar business elsewhere—and Mario would never be allowed to return to his own body.

He could follow the suggestion of the now disintegrated paper. No doubt Ralston Ebery had powerful political and financial connections, as well as great wealth in his own right. Or had he? Would it not be more likely that Ebery had liquidated as much of his wealth as possible, both to pay ten million dollars to the Chateau d'If, and also to provide his new body with financial backing?

Mario contemplated the use of force. There might be some means to compel the return of his body. Help would be useful. Should he report to Ditmar, Janniver, Breaugh? Indeed, he owed them some sort of explanation.

He rose to his feet. Mervyn Allen would not conceivably leave vulnerable areas in his defenses. He must realize that violence, revenge, would be the first idea in a mind shanghaied into an old sick body. There would be precautions against obvious violence, of that he was certain.

The ideas thronged, swirled, frothed, like different-colored paints stirred in a bucket. His head became light, a buzzing sounded in his ears. A dream, when would he awake? He gasped, panted, made feeble struggling motions. A patrolman stopped beside him, tripped his incident-camera automatically.

"What's wrong, sir? Taken sick?"

"No, no," said Mario. "I'm all right. Just dozed off."

He rose to his feet, stepped on the Choreops Strip, passed the central fountain flagged with aventurine quartz, stepped off at the Malabar Pavilion, wandered under the great bay trees out onto Kesselyn Avenue. Slowly, heavily, he plodded through the wholesale florist shops, and at Pacific, let the escalator take him to the third level, where he stepped on the fast pedestrip of the Grand Footway to the Concourse.

His progress had been unconscious, automatic, as if his body made the turns at their own volition. Now at the foot of the Aetherian Block he stepped off the strip, breathing a little heavily. The body of Ralston Ebery was spongy, in poor condition. And Mario felt an unholy gloating as he thought of Ralston Ebery's body sweating, puffing, panting, fasting—working off its lard.

A face suddenly thrust into his, a snarling hate-brimmed face. Teeth showed, the pupils of the eyes were like the black-tipped poison darts of the Mazumbwe Backlands. The face was that of a young-old man—unlined, but gray-haired; innocent but wise, distorted by the inner thrash and coil of his hate. Through tight teeth and corded jaw muscles the young-old man snarled:

"You filthy misbegotten dung-thief, do you hope to live? You venom, you stench. It would soil me to kill you. But I shall!"

Mario stepped back. The man was a stranger. "I'm sorry. You must be mistaken," he said, before it dawned that Ralston Ebery's deeds were now accountable to him.

A hand fell on the young-old man's shoulder. "Beat it, Arnold!" said a hard voice. "Be off with you!" The young-old man fell back.

Mario's rescuer turned around—a dapper young man with an agile fox-face. He nodded respectfully. "Good morning, Mr. Ebery. Sorry that crank bothered you."

"Good morning," said Mario. "Ah—who was he?"

The young man eyed him curiously. "Why, that's Letya Arnold. Used to work for us. You fired him."

Mario was puzzled. "Why?"

The young man blinked. "I'm sure I don't know. Inefficiency, I suppose."

"It's not important," said Mario hurriedly. "Forget it."

"Sure. Of course. On your way up to the office?"

"Yes, I—I suppose so." Who was this young man? It was a problem he would be called on to face many times, he thought.

They approached the elevators. "After you," said Mario. There was such an infinity of detail to be learned, a thousand personal adjustments, the intricate pattern of Ralston Ebery's business. Was there any business left? Ebery certainly would have plundered it of every cent he could endow his new body with. Ebery Air-car was a large concern; still the extracting of even ten million dollars was bound to make a dent. And this young man with the clever face, who was he? Mario decided to try indirectness, a vague question.

"Now let's see—how long since you've been promoted?"

The young man darted a swift side glance, evidently wondering whether Ebery was off his feed. "Why, I've been assistant office manager for two years."

Mario nodded. They stepped into the elevator, and the young man was quick to press the button. Obsequious cur! thought Mario. The door snapped shut, and there came the swoop which stomachs of the age had become inured to. The elevator halted, the doors flung back, they stepped out into a busy office, filled with clicking machinery, clerks, banks of telescreens. Clatter, hum—and sudden silence with every eye on the body of Ralston Ebery. Furtive glances, studied attentiveness to work, exaggerated efficiency.

Mario halted, looked the room over. It was his. By default. No one in the world could deny him authority over this concern, unless Ralston Ebery had been too fast, too greedy, raising his ten million plus. If Ralston Ebery had embezzled or swindled, he—Roland Mario in Ebery's body—would be punished. Mario was trapped in Ebery's past. Ebery's shortcomings would be held against him, the hate he had aroused would inflict itself on him, he had inherited Ebery's wife, his family, his mistress, if any.

A short middle-aged man with wide disillusioned eyes, the bitter clasp of mouth that told of many hopes lost or abandoned, approached.

"Morning, Mr. Ebery. Glad you're here. Several matters for your personal attention."

Mario looked sharply at the man. Was that overtone in his voice sarcasm? "In my office," said Mario. The short man turned toward a hallway. Mario followed. "Come along," he said to the assistant office manager.

Gothic letters wrought from silver spelled out Ralston Ebery's name on a door. Mario put his thumb into the lock; the prints meshed, the door slid aside; Mario slowly entered, frowning in distaste at the fussy *decor*. Ralston Ebery had been a lover of the rococo. He sat down behind the desk of polished black metal, said to the assistant office manager, "Bring me the personnel file on the office staff—records, photographs."

"Yes, sir."

The short man hauled a chair forward. "Now, Mr. Ebery, I'm sorry to say that I consider you've put the business in an ambiguous position."

"What do you mean?" asked Mario frostily, as if he were Ebery himself.

The short man snorted. "What do I mean? I mean that the

contracts you sold to Atlas Airboat were the biggest money-makers Ebery Air-car had. As you know very well. We took a terrible drubbing in that deal." The short man jumped to his feet, walked up and down. "Frankly, Mr. Ebery, I don't understand it."

"Just a minute," said Mario. "Let me look at the mail." Killing time, he thumbed through the mail until the assistant office manager returned with a file of cards.

"Thank you," said Mario. "That's all for now."

He flicked through them, glancing at the pictures. This short man had authority, he should be somewhere near the top. Here he was—Louis Correaos, Executive Adviser. Information as to salary, family, age, background—more than he could digest at the moment. He put the file to one side. Louis Correaos was still pacing up and down, fuming.

Correaos paused, darted Mario a venomous stare. "Ill-advised? I think you're crazy!" He shrugged. "I tell you this because my job means nothing to me. The company can't stand the beating you've given it. Not the way you want it run, at any rate. You insist on marketing a flying tea-wagon, festooned with ornaments; then you sell the only profitable contracts, the only features to the ship that make it at all airworthy."

Mario reflected a minute. Then he said, "I had my reasons."

Correaos, halting in his pacing, stared again.

Mario said, "Can you conjecture how I plan to profit from these circumstances?"

Correaos's eyes were like poker chips; his mouth contracted, tightened, pursed to an O. He was thinking. After a moment he said, "You sold our steel plant to Jones and Cahill, our patent on the ride stabilizer to Bluecraft." He gazed narrowly askance at Mario. "It sounds like you're doing what you swore you'd never do. Bring out a new model that would fly."

"How do you like the idea?" asked Mario, looking wise.

Louis Correaos stammered, "Why, Mr. Ebery, this is—fantastic! You asking *me* what *I* think! I'm your yes-man. That's what you're paying me for. I know it, you know it, everybody knows it."

"You haven't been yessing me today," said Ebery. "You told me I was crazy."

"Well," stammered Correaos, "I didn't see your idea. It's what I'd like to have done long ago. Put in a new transformer, pull off all that ormolu, use plancheen instead of steel, simplify, simplify—"

"Louis," said Mario, "make the announcement. Start the works rolling. You're in charge. I'll back up anything you want done."

Louis Correaos's face was a drained mask.

"Make your salary anything you want," said Mario. "I've got some new projects I'm going to be busy on. I want you to run the business. You're the boss. Can you handle it?"

"Yes. I can."

"Do it your own way. Bring out a new model that'll beat everything in the field. I'll check on the final set-up, but until then, you're the boss. Right now—clean up all this detail." He pointed to the file of correspondence. "Take it to your office."

Correaos impulsively rushed up, shook Mario's hand. "I'll do the best I can." He left the room.

Mario said into the communicator, "Get me the African Federal Bank. . . . Hello—" to the girl's face on the screen. "—this is Ralston Ebery. Please check on my personal balance."

After a moment she said, "It's down to twelve hundred dollars, Mr. Ebery. Your last withdrawal almost wiped out your balance."

"Thank you," said Mario. He settled the thick body of Ralston Ebery into the chair, and became aware of a great cavernous growling in his abdomen. Ralston Ebery was hungry.

Mario grinned a ghastly sour grin. He called food service. "Send up a chopped olive sandwich, celery, a glass of skim milk."

# CHAPTER V

## An Understanding

During the afternoon he became aware of an ordeal he could no longer ignore: acquainting himself with Ralston Ebery's family, his home life. It could not be a happy one. No happy husband and father would leave his wife and children at the mercy of a stranger. It was the act of hate, rather than love.

A group photograph stood on the desk—a picture inconspicuously placed, as if it were there on sufferance. This was his family. Florence Ebery was a frail woman, filmy, timid, over-dressed, and her face peering out from under a preposterous hat, wore the patient perplexed expression of a family pet dressed in doll clothes—somehow pathetic.

Luther and Ralston Jr. were stocky young men with set mulish faces, Clydia a full-cheeked creature with a petulant mouth.

At three o'clock Mario finally summoned up his courage, called Ebery's home on the screen, had Florence Ebery put on. She said in a thin distant voice, "Yes, Ralston."

"I'll be home this evening, dear." Mario added the last word with conscious effort.

She wrinkled her nose, pursed her lips and her eyes shone as if she were about to cry. "You don't even tell me where you've been."

Mario said, "Florence—frankly. Would you say I've been a good husband?"

She blinked defiantly at him. "I've no complaints. I've never complained." The pitch of her voice hinted that this perhaps was not literally true. Probably had reason, thought Mario.

"No, I want the truth, Florence."

"You've given me all the money I wanted. You've humiliated me a thousand times—snubbed me, made me a laughing stock for the children."

Mario said, "Well, I'm sorry, Florence." He could not vow affection. He felt sorry for Florence—Ebery's wife—but she was Ralston Ebery's wife, not his own. One of Ralston Ebery's victims. "See you this evening," he said lamely, and switched off.

He sat back. Think, think, think. There must be a way out. Or was this to be his life, his end, in this corpulent unhealthy body? Mario laughed suddenly. If ten million dollars bought Ralston Ebery a new body—presumably his own—then ten million more of Ralston Ebery's dollars might buy the body back. For money spoke a clear loud language to Mervyn Allen. Humiliating, a nauseous obsequious act, a kissing of the foot which kicked you, a submission, an acquiescence—but it was either this or wear the form of Ralston Ebery.

Mario stood up, walked to the window, stepped out on the landing plat, signaled down an aircab.

Ten minutes later he stood at 5600 Exmoor Avenue in Meadowlands, the Chateau d'If. A gardener clipping the hedges eyed him with distrust. He strode up the driveway, pressed the button.

There was, as before, a short wait, the unseen scrutiny of spy cells. The sun shone warm on his back, to his ears came the *shirrrrr* of the gardener's clippers.

The door opened.

"Please come in," said the soft commercial voice.

Down the hall, into the green and brown reception room with the painting of the three stark nudes before the olden forest.

The girl of fabulous beauty entered; Mario gazed again into the wide clear eyes which led to some strange brain. *Whose* brain? Mario wondered. Of man or woman?

No longer did Mario feel the urge to excite her, arouse her. She was unnatural, a *thing*.

"What do you wish?"

"I'd like to see Mr. Allen."

"On what business?"

"Ah, you know me?"

"On what business?"

"You're a money-making concern, are you not?"

"Yes."

"My business means money."

"Please be seated." She turned; Mario watched the slim body in retreat. She walked lightly, gracefully, in low elastic slippers. He became aware of Ebery's body. The old goat's glands were active enough. Mario fought down the wincing nausea.

The girl returned. "Follow me, please."

Mervyn Allen received him with affability, though not going so far as to shake hands.

"Hello, Mr. Mario. I rather expected you. Sit down. How's everything going? Enjoying yourself?"

"Not particularly. I'll agree that you've provided me with a very stimulating adventure. And indeed—now that I think back—nowhere have you made false representations."

Allen smiled a cool brief smile. And Mario wondered whose brain this beautiful body surrounded.

"Your attitude is unusually philosophical," said Allen. "Most of our customers do not realize that we give them exactly what they pay for. The essence of adventure is surprise, danger, and an outcome dependent upon one's own efforts."

"No question," remarked Mario, "that is precisely what you offer. But don't mistake me. If I pretended friendship, I would not be sincere. In spite of any rational processes, I feel a strong resentment. I would kill you without sorrow—even though, as you will point out, I brought the whole matter on myself."

"'Exactly."

"Aside from my own feelings, we have a certain community of interests, which I wish to exploit. You want money, I want my own body. I came to inquire by what circumstances our desires could both be satisfied."

Allen's face was joyous, he laughed delightedly. "Mario, you amuse me. I've heard many propositions, but none quite so formal, so elegant. Yes, I want money. You want the body you have become accustomed to. I'm sorry to say that your old body is now the property of someone else, and I doubt if he'd be persuaded to surrender it. But—I can sell you another body, healthy, handsome, young, for our usual fee. Ten million dollars. For thirty million I'll give you the widest possible choice—a body like mine, for instance. The Empyrean Tower is an exceedingly expensive project."

Mario said, "Out of curiosity, how is this transfer accomplished? I don't notice any scar or any sign of brain graft. Which in any event is probably impossible."

Mervyn Allen nodded. "It would be tedious, splicing several million sets of nerves. Are you acquainted with the physiology of the brain?"

"No," said Mario. "It's complicated, that's about all I know of it—or have cared to know."

Allen leaned back, relaxed, spoke rapidly, as if by rote. "The brain is divided into three parts, the medulla oblongata, the cerebellum—these two control involuntary motions and reflexes—and the cerebrum, the seat of memory, intelligence, personality. Thinking is done in the brain the same way thinking is done in mechanical brains, by the selection of a route through relays or neurons.

"In a blank brain, the relative ease of any circuit is the same, and the electric potential of each and every cell is the same.

"The process is divided into a series of steps—discovered, I may add, accidentally during a program of research in a completely different field. First, the patient's scalp is imbedded in a cellule of what the original research team called golasma—an organic crystal with a large number of peripheral fibers. Between the golasma cellule and the brain are a number of layers—hair, dermal tissue, bone, three separate membranes, as well as a mesh of blood vessels, very complicated. The neural cells however are unique in their high electric potential, and for practical purposes the intervening cells do not intrude.

"Next, by a complicated scanning process, we duplicate the synapses of the brain in the golasma, relating it by a pattern of sensory stimuli to a frame that will be common to all men.

"Third, the golasma cellules are changed, the process is reversed, A's brain is equipped with B's synapses, B with A's. The total process requires only a few minutes. Non-surgical, painless, harmless. A receives B's personality and memories, B takes on A's."

Slowly Mario rubbed his fat chin. "You mean, I—I—am not Roland Mario at all? That thinking Roland Mario's thoughts is an illusion? And not a cell in this body is Roland Mario?"

"Not the faintest breath. You're all—let me see. Your name is Ralston Ebery, I believe. Every last corpuscle of you is Ralston Ebery. You *are* Ralston Ebery, equipped with Roland Mario's memories."

"But, my glandular make-up? Won't it modify Roland Mario's personality? After all, a man's actions are not due to his brain alone, but to a synthesis of effects."

"Very true," said Allen. "The effect is progressive. You will gradually change, become like the Ralston Ebery before the change. And the same with Roland Mario's body. The total change will be determined by the environment against heredity ratio in your characters."

Mario smiled. "I want to get out of this body soon. What I see of Ebery I don't like."

"Bring in ten million dollars," said Mervyn Allen. "The Chateau d'If exists for one purpose—to make money."

Mario inspected Allen carefully, noted the hard clear flesh, the beautiful shape of the face, skull, expression.

"What do you *need* all that money for? Why build an Empyrean Tower in the first place?"

"I do it for fun. It amuses me. I am bored. I have explored many bodies, many existences. This body is my fourteenth. I've wielded power. I do not care for the sensation. The pressure annoys me. Nor am I at all psychotic. I am not even ruthless. In my business, what one man loses, another man gains. The balance is even."

"But it's robbery!" protested Mario bitterly. "Stealing the years off one man's life to add to another's."

Allen shrugged. "The bodies are living the same cumulative length of time. The total effect is the same. There's no change but the shifting of memory. In any event, perhaps I am, in the jargon of metaphysics, a solipsist. So far as I can see—through my eyes, through my brain—*I* am the only true individual, the sole conscious intellect." His eye shadowed. "How else can it be that I—I—have been chosen from among so many to lead this charmed life of mine?"

"Pooh!" sneered Mario.

"Every man amuses himself as best he knows how. My current interest is building the Empyrean Tower." His voice took on a deep exalted ring. "It shall rise three miles into the air! There is a banquet hall with a floor of alternate silver and copper strips, a quarter mile wide, a quarter mile high, ringed with eight glass balconies. There will be garden terraces like nothing else on earth, with fountains, waterfalls, running brooks. One floor will be a fairyland out of the ancient days, peopled with beautiful nymphs.

"Others will display Earth at stages in its history. There will be museums, conservatories of various musical styles, studios, workshops, laboratories for every known type of research, sections given to retail shops. There will be beautiful chambers and balconies designed for nothing except to be wandered through, sections devoted to the—let us say, worship of Astarte. There will be halls full of toys, a hundred restaurants staffed by gourmets, a thousand taverns serving liquid dreams; halls for seeing, hearing, resting."

Said Mario, "And after you tire of the Empyrean Tower?"

Mervyn Allen flung himself back in the seat. "Ah, Mario, you touch me on a sore point. Doubtless something will suggest itself. If only we could break away from Earth, could fly past the barren rocks of the planets, to other stars, other life. There would be no need for any Chateau d'If."

Mario rubbed his fat jowl, eyed Allen quizzically. "Did you invent this process yourself?"

"I and four others who comprised a research team. They are all dead. I alone know the technique."

"And your secretary? Is she one of your changelings?"

"No," said Mervyn Allen. "Thane is what she is. She lives by hate. You think I am her lover? No," and he smiled faintly. "Not in any way. Her will is for destruction, death. A bright thing only on the surface. Inwardly she is as dark and violent, as a drop of hot oil."

Mario had absorbed too many facts, too much information. He was past speculating. "Well, I won't take any more of your time. I wanted to find out where I stand."

"Now you know. I need money. This is the easiest way to get it in large quantities that I know of. But I also have my big premium offer—bank night, bingo, whatever you wish to call it."

"What's that?"

"I need customers. The more customers, the more money. Naturally my publicity cannot be too exact. So I offer a free shift, a free body if you bring in six new customers."

Mario narrowed his eyes. "So—Sutlow gets credit for Zaer and me?"

Allen looked blank. "Who's Sutlow?"

"You don't know Sutlow?"

"Never heard of him."

"How about Ditmar?"

"Ah, he's successful, is Ditmar. Ten thousand bought him a body with advanced cirrhosis. Two more customers and he escapes. But perhaps I talk too much. I can give you no more time, Mario. Good night."

On his way out, Mario stopped in the reception room, looked down into the face of Thane. She stared back, a face like stone, eyes like star sapphires. Mario suddenly felt exalted, mystic, as if he walked on live thought, knew the power of insight.

"You're beautiful but you're cold as the sea-bed."

"This door will take you out, sir."

"Your beauty is so new and so fragile a thing—a surface only a millimeter thick. Two strokes of a knife would make you a horrible sight, one from which people would look aside as you pass."

She opened her mouth, closed it, rose to her feet, said, "This way out, sir."

Mario reached, caught sight of Ralston Ebery's fat flaccid fingers, grimaced, pulled back his hands. "I could not touch you—with these hands."

"Nor with any others," she said from the cool distance of her existence.

He passed her to the door. "If you see the most beautiful creature that could possibly exist, if she has a soul like rock crystal, if she challenges you to take her, break her, and you are lost in a fat hideous porridge of a body—"

Her expression shifted a trifle, in which direction he could not tell. "This is the Chateau d'If," she said. "And you *are* a fat hideous porridge."

He wordlessly departed. She slid the door shut. Mario shrugged, but Ralston Ebery's face burnt in a hot glow of humiliation. There was no love, no thought of love. Nothing more than the challenge, much like the dare of a mountain to the climbers who scale its height, plunder the secrets of its slopes, master the crest. Thane, cold as the far side of the moon!

Get away, said Mario's brain sharply, break clear of the obsession. Fluff, female bodies, forget them. Is not the tangle of enough complexity?

# CHAPTER VI

## *Leverage*

From the door of the Chateau d'If Mario took an aircab to 19 Seafoam Place—a monster house of pink marble, effulgent, voluted, elaborate as the rest of Ralston Ebery's possessions. He thumbed the lock-hole. The prints meshed with identification patterns, the door snapped back. Mario entered.

The photograph had prepared him for his family. Florence Ebery greeted him with furtive suspicion; the sons were blank, passively hostile. The daughter seemed to have no emotions whatever, other than a constant air of puzzled surprise.

At dinner, Mario outraged Ebery's body by eating nothing but a salad of lettuce, carrots and vinegar. His family was puzzled.

"Are you feeling well, Ralston?" inquired his wife.

"Very well."

"You're not eating."

"I'm dieting. I'm going to take the lard off this hideous body."

Eight eyes bulged, four sets of knives and forks froze.

Mario went on placidly, "We're going to have some changes around here. Too much easy living is bad for a person." He addressed himself to the two young men, both alike with white faces, doughy cheeks, full lips. "You lads now—I don't want to be hard on you. After all, it's not your fault you were born Ralston Ebery's sons. But do you know what it means to earn a living by sweating for it?"

Luther, the eldest, spoke with dignity. "We work with the sweat of our brains."

"Tell me more about it," said Mario.

Luther's eyes showed anger. "I put out more work in one week than you do all year."

"Where?"

"Where? Why, in the glass yard. Where else?" There was fire here, more than Mario had expected.

Ralston Jr. said in a gruff surly voice, "We're paying you our board and room, we don't owe you a red cent. If you don't like the arrangements the way they are, we'll leave."

Mario winced. He had misjudged Ebery's sons. White faces, doughy cheeks, did not necessarily mean white doughy spirits. Better keep his opinions to himself, base his conversation on known fact. He said mildly, "Sorry, I didn't mean to offend you. Forget the board and room. Spend it on something useful."

He glanced skeptically toward Clydia, Ebery's daughter. She half-simpered. Better keep his mouth shut. She might turn out to be a twelve-hour-a-day social service worker.

Nevertheless, Mario found himself oppressed in Ebery's house. Though living in Ebery's body, the feel of his clothes, his intimate equipment was profoundly disturbing. He could not bring himself to use Ebery's razor or toothbrush. Attending to the needs of Ebery's body was most exquisitely distasteful. He discovered to his relief that his bedroom was separate from that of Florence Ebery.

He arose the next morning very early, scarcely after dawn, hurriedly left the house, breakfasted on orange juice and dry toast at a small restaurant. Ebery's stomach protested the meager rations with angry rumbling. Ebery's legs complained when Mario decided to walk the pedestrip instead of calling down an aircab.

He let himself into the deserted offices of Ebery Air-car, wandered absently back and forth the length of the suite, thinking. Still thinking, he let himself into his private office. The clutter, the rococo junk, annoyed him. He called up a janitor, waved his hand around the room. "Clear out all this fancy stuff. Take it home, keep it. If you don't want it, throw it away. Leave me the desk, a couple of chairs. The rest— out!"

He sat back, thinking. Ways, means.

What weapons could he use?

He drew marks on a sheet of paper.

How could he attack?

Perhaps the law could assist him—somehow. Perhaps the ACP. But what statute did Mervyn Allen violate? There were no precedents. The Chateau d'If sold adventure. If a customer bought a great deal more than he had bargained for, he had only himself to blame.

Money, money, money. It could not buy back his own body. He needed leverage, a weapon, pressure to apply.

He called the public information service, requested the file on "golasma." It was unknown.

He drew more marks, scribbled meaningless patterns, where was Mervyn Allen vulnerable? The Chateau d'If, the Empyrean Tower. Once more he dialed into the public information service, requested the sequence on the Empyrean Tower. Typescript flashed across his screen.

> The Empyrean Tower will be a multiple-function building at a site in Meadowlands. The highest level will be three miles above ground. The architects are Kubal Associates, Incorporated, of Lanchester. Foundation contracts have been let to Lourey and Lyble—"

Mario touched the shift button; the screen showed an architect's pencil sketch—a slender structure pushing through cloud layers into the clear blue sky. Mario touched the shift button.

Now came detailed information, as to the weight, cubic volume, comparison with the Pyramids, the Chilung Gorge Dam, the Skatterholm complex at Ronn, the Hawke Pylon, the World's Mart at Dar es Salaam.

Mario pushed at his communicator button. No answer. Still too early. Impatient now, he ordered coffee, drank two cups, pacing the office nervously.

At last a voice answered his signal. "When Mr. Correaos comes in, I'd like to speak to him."

Five minutes later Louis Correaos knocked at his door.

" 'Morning, Louis," said Mario.

"Good morning, Mr. Ebery," said Correaos with a tight guarded expression, as if expecting the worst.

Mario said, "Louis, I want some advice . . . have you ever heard of Kubal Associates, Incorporated? Architects?"

"No. Can't say as I have."

"I don't want to distract you from your work," said Mario,

"but I want to acquire control of that company. Quietly. Secretly, even. I'd like you to make some quiet inquiries. Don't use my name. Buy up as much voting stock as is being offered. Go as high as you like, but get the stock. And don't use my name."

Correaos's face became a humorous mask, with a bitter twist to his mouth. "What am I supposed to use for money?"

Mario rubbed the flabby folds around his jaw. *"Hm.* There's no reserve fund, no bank balance?"

Correaos looked at him queerly.

"You should know."

Mario squinted off to the side. True, he should know. To Louis Correaos, this was Ralston Ebery sitting before him—the arbitrary, domineering Ralston Ebery. Mario said, "Check on how much we can raise, will you, Louis?"

Correaos said, "Just a minute." He left the room. He returned with a bit of paper.

"I've been figuring up retooling costs. We'll have to borrow. It's none of my business what you did with the fund."

Mario smiled grimly. "You'd never understand, Louis. And if I told you, you wouldn't believe me. Just forget it. It's gone."

"The South African agency sent a draft for a little over a million yesterday. That won't even touch retooling."

Mario made an impatient gesture. "We'll get a loan. Right now you've got a million. See how much of Kubal Associates you can buy."

Correaos left the room without a word. Mario muttered to himself, "Thinks I'm off my nut. Figures he'll humor me. . . ."

All morning Mario turned old files through his desk-screen, trying to catch the thread of Ebery's business. There was much evidence of Ebery's hasty plundering—the cashing of bonds, disposal of salable assets, transference of the depreciation funds into his personal account. But in spite of the pillaging, Ebery Air-car seemed financially sound. It held mortgages, franchises, contracts worth many times what cash Ebery had managed to clear.

Tiring of the files, he ordered more coffee, paced the floor. His mind turned to 19 Seafoam Place. He thought of the accusing eyes of Florence Ebery, the hostility of Luther and Ralston Jr. And Mario wished Ralston Ebery a place in hell. Ebery's family was no responsibility, no concern of his. He called Florence Ebery.

"Florence, I won't be living at home any more." He tried to speak kindly.

She said, "That's what I thought."

Mario said hurriedly, "I think that, by and large, you'd be better off with a divorce. I won't contest it; you can have as much money as you want."

She gave him a fathomless silent stare. "That's what I thought," she said again. The screen went dead.

Correaos returned shortly after lunch. It was warm, Correaos had walked the pedestrip, his face shone with perspiration.

He flung a carved black plastic folder on the desk, baring his teeth in a triumphant smile. "There it is. I don't know what you want with it, but there it is. Fifty-two percent of the stock. I bought it off of old man Kubal's nephew and a couple of the associates. Got 'em at the right time; they were glad to sell. They don't like the way the business is going. Old man Kubal gives all his time to the Empyrean Tower, and he's not taking any fee for the work. Says the honor of the job is enough. The nephew doesn't dare to fight it out with old man Kubal, but he sure was glad to sell out. The same with Kohn and Cheever, the associates. The Empyrean Tower job doesn't even pay the office overhead."

"*Hm.* How old is Kubal?"

"Must be about eighty. Lively old boy, full of vinegar."

Honor of the job! thought Mario. Rubbish! Old Kubal's fee would be a young body. Aloud he said, "Louis, have you ever seen Kubal?"

"No, he hardly shows his face around the office. He lines up the jobs, the engineering is done in the office."

"Louis," said Mario, "here's what I want you to do. Record the stock in your own name, give me an undated transfer, which we won't record. You'll legally control the firm. Call the office, get hold of the general manager. Tell him that you're sending me over. I'm just a friend of yours you owe a favor to. Tell him that I'm to be given complete and final authority over any job I decide to work on. Get it?"

Correaos eyed Mario as if he expected the fat body to explode into fire. "Anything you like. I suppose you know what you're doing."

Mario grinned ruefully. "I can't think of anything else to do. In the meantime, bring out your new model. You're in charge."

Mario dressed Ralston Ebery's body in modest blue, reported to the office of Kubal Associates, an entire floor in the Rothenburg Building. He asked the receptionist for the manager and was shown in to a tall man in the early forties with a delicate lemonish face. He had a freckled forehead, thin sandy hair, and he answered Mario's questions with sharpness and hostility.

"My name is Taussig. . . . No, I'm just the office manager. Kohn ran the draughting room, Cheever the engineering. They're both out. The office is a mess. I've been here twelve years."

Mario assured him that there was no intention of stepping in over him. "No, Mr. Taussig, you're in charge. I speak for the new control. You handle the office—general routine, all the new jobs—just as usual. Your title is general manager. I want to work on the Empyrean Tower—without any interference. I won't bother you, you won't bother me. Right? After the Empyrean Tower, I leave and the entire office is yours."

Taussig's face unwound from around the lines of suspicion. "There's not much going on except the Empyrean Tower. Naturally that's a tremendous job in itself. Bigger than any one man."

Mario remarked that he did not expect to draw up the entire job on his own bench, and Taussig's face tightened again, at the implied sarcasm. No, said Mario, he merely would be the top ranking authority on the job, subject only to the wishes of the builder.

"One last thing," said Mario. "This talk we've had must be," he tilted Taussig a sidelong wink, "strictly confidential. You'll introduce me as a new employee, that's all. No word of the new control. No word of his being a friend of mine. Forget it. Get me?"

Taussig agreed with sour dignity.

"I want quiet," said Mario thoughtfully. "I want no contact with any of the principals. The interviews with the press— you handle those. Conferences with the builder, changes, modifications—you attend to them. I'm merely in the background."

"Just as you say," said Taussig.

# CHAPTER VII

## *Empyrean Tower*

Empyrean Tower became as much a part of Mario's life as his breath, his pulse. Twelve hours a day, thirteen, fourteen, Ebery's fat body sat slumped at the long desk, and Ebery's eyes burned and watered from poring through estimates, details, floor plans. On the big screen four feet before his eyes flowed the work of twenty-four hundred draughtsmen, eight hundred engineers, artists, decorators, craftsmen without number, everything subject to his approval. But his influence was restrained, nominal, unnoticed. Only in a few details did Mario interfere, and then so carefully, so subtly, that the changes were unknown.

The new building techniques, the control over material, the exact casting of plancheen and allied substances, prefabrication, effortless transport of massive members made the erection of the Empyrean Tower magically easy and swift. Level by level it reached into the air, growing like a macrocosmic bean sprout. Steel, concrete, plancheen floors and walls, magnesium girders, outriggers, buttresses, the new bubble glass for windows—assembled into precise units, hoisted, dropped into place from freight copters.

All day and all night the blue glare of the automatic welders burnt the sky, and sparks spattered against the stars, and every day the aspiring bulk pushed closer to the low clouds. Then through the low clouds, up toward the upper levels. Sun at one stage, rain far below. Up mile after mile, into the regions of air where the wind always swept like cream, undisturbed, unalloyed with the warm fetor of earth.

Mario was lost in the Empyrean Tower. He knew the range of materials, the glitter of a hundred metals, the silky gloss of plancheen, the color of the semi-precious minerals: jade, cinnabar, malachite, agate, jet, rare porphyries from under the Antarctic ranges. Mario forgot himself, forgot the Chateau d'If, forgot Mervyn Allen, Thane, Louis Correaos and Ebery Air-car, except for spasmodic, disassociated spells when he tore himself away from the Rothenburg Building for a few hours.

And sometimes, when he would be most engrossed, he would find to his horror that his voice, his disposition, his mannerisms were not those of Roland Mario. Ralston Ebery's lifelong reflexes and habits were making themselves felt. And Roland Mario felt a greater urgency. Build, build, build!

And nowhere did Mario work more carefully than on the 900th level—the topmost floor, noted on the index as offices and living quarters for Mervyn Allen. With the most intricate detail did Mario plan the construction, specifying specially-built girders, ventilating equipment, all custom-made to his own dimensions.

And so months in Mario's life changed their nature from future to past, months during which he became almost accustomed to Ralston Ebery's body.

On a Tuesday night Mario's personality had been fitted into Ralston Ebery's body. Wednesday morning he had come to his senses. Friday he was deep in concentration at the office of Ebery Air-car in the Aetherian Block, and three o'clock passed without his awareness. Friday evening he thought of the Oxonian Terrace, his rendezvous with Janniver, Breaugh, the nameless spirit in the sick body named Ditmar. And the next Tuesday at three, Mario was sitting at a table on the Oxonian Terrace.

Twenty feet away sat Janniver, Breaugh, Ditmar. And Mario thought back to the day only a few weeks ago when the five sat lackadaisically in the sun. Four innocents and one man eyeing them hungrily, weighing the price their bodies would bring.

Two of those bodies he had won. And Mario saw them sitting quietly in the warm sunlight, talking slowly—two of them, at least, peaceful and secure. Breaugh spoke with the customary cocksure tilt to his dark head, Janniver was slow and sober, an odd chording of racial vibrants. And there was Ditmar, a foreign soul looking sardonically from the lean dark-bronze body. A sick body, that a man paying ten thousand dollars for adventure would consider a poor bargain. Ditmar had bought adventure—an adventure in pain and fear. For a moment Mario's flinty mood loosened enough to admit that in yearning for his old own life in his old own body, a man might easily forget decency, fairness. The drowning man strangles a would-be rescuer.

Mario sipped beer indecisively. Should he join the three? It could do no harm. He was detained by a curious reluctance, urgent, almost a sense of shame. To speak to these men, tell them what their money had bought him—Mario felt the warm stickiness, the internal crawling of extreme embarrassment. At sudden thought, Mario scanned the nearby tables. Zaer. He had almost forgotten Pete Zaer. A millionaire's mind lived in Zaer's body. Would Zaer's mind bring the millionaire's body here?

Mario saw an old man with hollow eyes alone at a nearby table. Mario stared, watched his every move. The old man lit a cigarette, puffed, flicked the match—one of Zaer's tricks. The cigarette between his fingers, he lifted his highball, drank, once, twice put the cigarette in his mouth, set the glass down. Zaer's mannerism.

Mario rose, moved, took a seat. The old man looked up eagerly, then angrily, from dry red-rimmed eyes. The skin was a calcined yellow, the mouth was gray. Zaer had bought even less for his money than Mario.

"Is your name Pete Zaer?" asked Mario. "In disguise?"

The old man's mouth worked. The eyes swam. "How— Why do you say that?"

Mario said, "Look at the table. Who else is missing?"

"Roland Mario," said the old man in a thin rasping voice. The red eyes peered. *"You!"*

"That's right," said Mario, with a sour grin. "In a week or two maybe there'll be three of us, maybe four." He motioned. "Look at them. What are they shaking dice for?"

"We've got to stop them," rasped Zaer. "They don't *know*." But he did not move. Nor did Mario. It was like trying to make himself step naked out upon a busy street.

Something rigid surrounded, took hold of Mario's brain. He stood up. "You wait here," he muttered. "I'll try to put a stop to it."

He ambled across the sun-drenched terrace, to the table where Janniver was rolling dice. Mario reached his hands down, caught up the meaningful cubes.

Janniver looked up with puzzled eyes. Breaugh bent his straight Welsh eyebrows in the start of a temper. Ditmar, frowning, leaned back.

"Excuse me," said Mario. "May I ask what you're rolling for?"

Breaugh said, "A private matter. It does not concern you."

"Does it concern the Chateau d'If?"

Six eyes stared.

"Yes," said Breaugh, after a second or two of hesitation.

Mario said, "I'm a friend of Roland Mario's. I have a message from him."

"What is it?"

"He said to stay away from the Chateau d'If; not to waste your money. He said not to trust anyone who suggested for you to go there."

Breaugh snorted. "Nobody's suggesting anything to anybody."

"And he says he'll get in touch with you soon."

Mario left without formality, returned to where he had left Zaer. The old man with the hot red eyes was gone.

Ralston Ebery had many enemies, so Mario found. There were a large number of acquaintances, no friends. And there was one white-faced creature that seemed to live only to waylay him, hiss vileness. This was Letya Arnold, a former employee in the research laboratories.

Mario ignored the first and second meetings, and on the third he told the man to keep out of his way. "Next time I'll call the police."

"Filth-tub," gloated Arnold. "You wouldn't dare! The publicity would ruin you, and you know it, you know it!"

Mario inspected the man curiously. He was clearly ill. His breath reeked of internal decay. Under a loose gray-brown jacket his chest was concave, his shoulders pushed forward like doorknobs. His eyes were a curious shiny black, so black that the pupils were indistinguishable from the iris, and the eyes looked like big black olives pressed into two bowls of sour milk.

"There's a patrolman now," said Arnold. "Call him, mucknose, call him!"

Quickly Mario turned, walked away, and Arnold's laughter rang against his back.

Mario asked Louis Correaos about Letya Arnold. "Why wouldn't I dare have him arrested?"

And Correaos turned on him one of his long quizzical stares. "Don't you know?"

Mario remembered that Correaos thought he was Ebery. He rubbed his forehead. "I'm forgetful, Louis. Tell me about Letya Arnold."

"He worked in the radiation lab, figured out some sort of process that saved fuel. We naturally had a legal right to the patent." Correaos smiled sardonically. "Naturally we didn't use the process, since you owned stock in World Air-Power, and a big block of Lamarr Atomics. Arnold began unauthorized use. We took it to court, won, recovered damages. It put Arnold into debt and he hasn't been worth anything since."

Mario said with sudden energy, "Let me see that patent, Louis."

Correaos spoke into the mesh and a minute later a sealed envelope fell out of the slot into the catch-all.

Correaos said idly, "Myself, I think Arnold was either crazy or a fake. The idea he had couldn't work. Like perpetual motion."

Letya Arnold had written a short preface to the body of the paper, this latter a mass of circuits and symbols unintelligible to Mario.

The preface read:

> Efficiency in propulsion is attained by expelling ever smaller masses at ever higher velocities. The limit, in the first case, is the electron. Expelling it at speeds approaching that of light, we find that its mass increases by the well-known effect. This property provides us a perfect propulsive method, capable of freeing flight from its dependence upon heavy loads of material to be ejected at relatively slow velocities. One electron magnetically repelled at near-light speeds, exerts as much forward recoil as many pounds of conventional fuel. . . .

Mario knew where to find Letya Arnold. The man sat brooding day after day in Tanagra Square, on a bench beside the Centennial Pavilion. Mario stopped in front of him, a young-old man with a hysterical face.

Arnold looked up, arose eagerly, almost as if he would assault Mario physically.

Mario in a calm voice said, "Arnold, pay attention a minute. You're right, I'm wrong."

Arnold's face hung slack as a limp bladder. Attack needs resistance on which to harden itself. Feebly his fury asserted itself. He reeled off his now-familiar invective. Mario listened a minute.

"Arnold, the process you invented—have you ever tested it in practice?"

"Of course, you swine. Naturally. Of course. What do you take me for? One of your blow-hard call-boys?"

"It works, you say. Now listen, Arnold: we're working on a new theory at Ebery Air-car. We're planning to put out value at low cost. I'd like to build your process into the new model. If it actually does what you say. And I'd like to have you come back to work for us."

Letya Arnold snorted, his whole face a gigantic sneer. "Put that propulsion into an air-boat? *Pah!* Use a drop-forge to kill a flea? Where's your head, where's your head? It's space-drive; that's where we're going. Space!"

It was Mario's turn to be taken aback. "Space? Will it work in space?" he asked weakly.

"Work? It's just the thing! You took all my money—you!" The words were like skewers, dripping an acrid poison. "If I had my money now, patent or no patent, I'd be out in space. I'd be ducking around Alpha Centauri, Sirius, Vega, Capella!"

The man was more than half-mad, thought Mario. He said, "You can't go faster than light."

Letya Arnold's voice became calm, crafty. "Who said I can't? You don't know the things I know, swine-slut."

Mario said, "No, I don't. But all that aside, I'm a changed man, Arnold. I want you to forget any injustice I may have done you. I want you back at work for Ebery Air-car. I'd like you to adapt the drive for public use."

Again Arnold sneered. "And kill everything that happened to be behind you? Every electron shot from the reactor would be like a meteor; there'd be blasts of incandescent air; impact like a cannon-ball. No, no—space. That's where the drive must go. . . ."

"You're hired, if you want to be," said Mario patiently. "The laboratory's waiting for you. I want you to work on that adaptation. There must be some kind of shield." Noting the taut clamp to Arnold's mouth, he said hastily, "If you think you can go faster than light, fine! Build a ship for space and I'll test fly it myself. But put in your major effort on the adaptation for public use, that's all I ask."

Arnold, cooler by the minute, now exhibited the same kind of sardonic unbelief Mario had noticed in Correaos. "Blow me, but you've changed your tune, Ebery. Before it was money, money, money. If it didn't make you money, plow it under. What happened to you?"

"The Chateau d'If," said Mario. "If you value your sanity, don't go there. Though God knows," and he looked at Arnold's wasted body, "you couldn't do much worse for yourself than you've already done."

"If it changes me as much as it's changed you, I'm giving it a wide berth. Blow me, but you're almost human."

"I'm a changed man," said Mario. "Now go to Correaos, get an advance, go to a doctor."

On his way to the Rothenburg Building and Kubal Associates it came to him to wonder how Ebery was using his body. In his office he ran down a list of detective agencies, settled on Brannan Investigators, called them, put them to work.

# CHAPTER VIII

## *Inventor With a Grudge*

Investigator Murris Slade, the detective, was a short thick-set man with a narrow head. Two days after Mario had called the Brannan agency, he knocked at Mario's workroom at Kubal Associates.

Mario looked through the wicket in the locked door, admitted the detective, who said without preamble, "I've found your man."

"Good," said Mario, returning to his seat. "What's he doing?"

Slade said, in a quiet accentless voice, "There's no mystery or secrecy involved. He seems to have changed his way of living in the last few months. I understand he was quite a chap, pretty well-liked, nothing much to set him apart. One of the idle rich. Now he's a hell-raiser, a woman-chaser, and he's been thrown out of every bar in town."

My poor body, thought Mario. Aloud: "Where's he living?"

"He's got an apartment at the Atlantic-Empire, fairly plush place. It's a mystery where he gets his money."

The Atlantic-Empire seemed to have become a regular rendezvous for Chateau d'If alumni, thought Mario. He said, "I want a weekly report on this man. Nothing complicated—just a summary of where he spends his time. Now, I've got another job for you. . . ."

The detective reported on the second job a week later.

"Mervyn Allen is an alias. The man was born Lloyd Paren, in Vienna. The woman is his sister, Thane Paren. Originally he was a photographer's model, something of a playboy—up until a few years ago. Then he came into a great deal of money. Now, as you probably know, he runs the Chateau d'If. I can't get anything on that. There's rumors, but anybody that knows anything won't talk. The rumors are not in accord with Paren's background, which is out in the open—no medical or psychosomatic training. The woman was originally a music student, a specialist in primitive music. When Paren left Vienna, she came with him. Paren lives at 5600 Exmoor Avenue—that's the Chateau d'If. Thane Paren lives in a little apartment about a block away, with an old man, no relative. Neither one seems to have any intimate friends, and there's no entertaining, no parties. Not much to go on."

Mario reflected a few moments, somberly gazing out the window, while Murris Slade sat impassively waiting for Mario's instructions. At last Mario said, "Keep at it. Get some more on the old man Thane Paren lives with."

One day Correaos called Mario on the telescreen. "We've got the new model blocked out." He was half-placating, half-challenging, daring Mario to disapprove of his work.

"I think we've done a good job," said Correaos. "You wanted to give it a final check."

"I'll be right over," said Mario.

The new model had been built by hand at the Donnic River Plant and flown into Lanchester under camouflage. Correaos managed the showing as if Mario were a buyer, in whom he was trying to whip up enthusiasm.

"The idea of this model—I've tentatively called it the Airfarer—was to use materials which were plain and cheap, dispense with all unnecessary ornament—which, in my opinion, has been the bane of the Ebery Air-car. We've put the savings into clean engineering, lots of room, safety. Notice the lift vanes, they're recessed, almost out of reach. No drunk is going to walk into them. Those pulsors, they're high, and the deflection jets are out of reach. The frame and fuselage are solid cast plancheen, first job like this in the business."

Mario listened, nodded appreciatively from time to time. Apparently Correaos had done a good job. He asked, "How about what's-his-name—Arnold? Has he come up with anything useful?"

Correaos bared his teeth, clicked his tongue. "That man's crazy. He's a walking corpse. All he thinks, all he talks, are his pestiferous electrons, what he calls a blast effect. I saw a demonstration, and I think he's right. We can't use it in a family vehicle."

"What's the jet look like?"

Correaos shrugged. "Nothing much. A generator—centaurium powered—a miniature synchrotron. Very simple. He feeds a single electron into the tube, accelerates it to the near-light speed, and it comes roaring out in a gush as thick as your arm."

Mario frowned. "Try to steer him back onto something useful. He's got the brains. Has he been to a doctor?"

"Just Stapp, the insurance doctor. Stapp says it's a wonder he's alive now. Galloping nephritis or necrosis—some such thing." Correaos spoke without interest. His eyes never left his new Airfarer. He said with more life in his voice, "Look into the interior, notice the wide angle of vision; also the modulating glare filter. Look right up into the sun, all you want. Notice the altimeter, it's got a positive channel indicator, that you can set for any given locality. Then the pressurizer, it's built in under the rear seat—see it?—saves about twenty dollars a unit over the old system. Instead of upholstery, I've had the framework machined smooth, and sprayed it with sprinjufloss."

"You've done a good job, Louis," said Mario. "Go ahead with it."

Correaos took a deep breath, released it, shook his head. "I'll be dyed-double-and-throttled!"

"What's the trouble?"

"I don't get you at all," said Correaos, staring at Mario as if he were a stranger. "If I didn't know you stem to stern, I'd say you were a different man. Three months ago, if I'd tried to put something cleanly designed in front of you, you'd have gone off like one of Arnold's electrons. You'd have called this job a flying bread-box. You'd have draped angel's-wings all over the outside, streamlined the dashboard fixtures, built in two or three Louis Fifteenth book cases. I don't know whatall. If you didn't look so healthy, I'd say you were sick."

Mario said with an air of sage deliberation, "Ebery Air-car has taken a lot of money out of the public. The old Ebery managed to keep itself in the air, but it cost a lot and looked like a pagoda on wings. Now we'll start giving 'em quality. Maybe they'll turn it down."

Correaos laughed exultantly. "If we can't sell ten million of these, I'll run one up as high as she'll go and jump."

"Better start selling, then."

"I hope you don't have a relapse," said Correaos, "and order a lot of fancy fittings."

"No," said Mario mildly. "She'll go out just as she is, so long as I have anything to say about it."

Correaos slapped the hull of the Airfarer approvingly, turned a quizzical face to Mario. "Your wife has been trying to get in touch with you. I told her I didn't know where you were. You'd better call her—if you want to stay married. She was talking about divorce."

Mario looked off into the distance, uncomfortably aware of Correaos's scrutiny. "I told her to go ahead with it. It's the best thing for everybody concerned. Fairest for her, at any rate."

Correaos shook his head. "You're a funny fellow, Ebery. A year ago you'd have fired me a dozen times over."

"Maybe I'm getting you fat for the slaughter," suggested Mario.

"Maybe," said Correaos. "Letya Arnold and I can go into business making electron elephant guns."

Two hundred thousand artisans swarmed over the Tower, painting, plastering, spraying, fitting in pipes, wires, pouring terazzo, concrete, plancheen, installing cabinets, a thousand kinds of equipment. Walls were finished with panels of waxed and polished woods, the myriad pools were tiled, the gardeners landscaped the hanging parks, the great green bowers in the clouds.

Every week Mervyn Allen conferred with Taussig and old man Kubal, approving, modifying, altering, canceling, expanding. From recorded copies of the interviews Mario worked, making the changes Allen desired, meshing them carefully into his own designs.

Months passed. Now Mervyn Allen might not have recognized this man as Ralston Ebery. At the Ebery Air-car office in the Aetherian Block, his employees were astounded, respectful. It was a new Ralston Ebery—though, to be sure, they noticed the old gestures, the tricks of speech, habits of walking, dressing, involuntary expressions. This new Ralston Ebery had sloughed away fifty pounds of oil and loose flesh. The sun had tinted the white skin to a baby pink. The eyes, once puffy, now shone out of meaty cheeks; the leg muscles were tough with much walking; the chest was deeper, the lungs stronger from the half-hour of swimming every afternoon at four o'clock.

And at last the two hundred thousand artisans packed their tools, collected their checks. Maintenance men came on the job. Laborers swept, scrubbed, polished. The Empyrean Tower was complete—a solidified dream, a wonder of the world. A building rising like a pine tree, supple and massive, overbounding the minuscule streets and squares below. An edifice not intended for grace, yet achieving grace through its secure footing, its incalculable tapers, set-backs, thousand terraces, thousand taxiplats, million windows.

The Empyrean Tower was completed. Mervyn Allen moved in on a quiet midnight, and the next day the Chateau d'If at 5600 Exmoor Avenue, Meadowlands, was vacant, for sale or for lease.

The Chateau d'If was now Level 900, Empyrean Tower. And Roland Mario ached with eagerness, anxiety, a hot gladness intense to the point of lust. He was slowly cleaning off his desk when Taussig poked his head into the office.

"Well, what are you planning to do now?"

Mario inspected Taussig's curious face. "Any more big jobs?"

"Nope. And not likely to be. At least not through old man Kubal."

"How come? Has he retired?"

"Retired? Shucks, no. He's gone crazy. Schizo."

Mario drummed his fingers on his desk. "When did all this happen?"

"Just yesterday. Seems like finishing the Empyrean was too much for him. A cop found him in Tanagra Square talking to himself, took him home. Doesn't know his nephew, doesn't know his housekeeper. Keeps saying his name is Bray, something like that."

"Bray?" Mario rose to his feet, his forehead knotting. Breaugh. "Sounds like senile decay," he said abstractedly.

"That's right," Taussig responded, still fixing Mario with bright curious eyes. "So what are you going to do now?"

"I quit," said Mario, with an exaggerated sweep of the arm. "I'm done, I'm like old man Kubal. The Empyrean Tower's too much for me. I've got senile decay. Take a good look, Taussig, you'll never see me again." He closed the door in Taussig's slack face. He stepped into the elevator, dropped to the second level, hopped the high-speed strip to his small apartment at Melbourne House. He thumbed the lock, the scanner recognized his prints, the door slid back. Mario entered, closed the door. He undressed Ebery's gross body, wrapped it in a robe, sank with a grunt into a chair beside a big low table.

The table held a complex model built of wood, metal, plastic, vari-colored threads. It represented Level 900, Empyrean Tower—the Chateau d'If.

Mario knew it by heart. Every detail of an area a sixth of a mile square was pressed into his brain.

Presently Mario dressed again, in coveralls of hard gray twill. He loaded his pockets with various tools and equipment, picked up his handbag. He looked at himself in the mirror, at the face that was Ebery and yet not quite Ebery. The torpid glaze had left the eyes. The lips were no longer puffy, the jowls had pulled up, his face was a meaty slab. Thoughtfully Mario pulled a cap over his forehead, surveyed the effect. The man was unrecognizable. He attached a natty wisp of mustache. Ralston Ebery no longer existed.

Mario left the apartment. He hailed a cab, flew out to Meadowlands. The Empyrean Tower reared over the city like a fence post standing over a field of cabbages. An aircraft beacon scattered red rays from a neck-twisting height. A million lights from nine hundred levels glowed, blended into a rich milky shimmer. A city in itself, where two million, three million men and women might live their lives out if they so wished. It was a monument to the boredom of one man, a man sated with life. The most magnificent edifice ever built, and built for the least consequential of motives that ever caused one rock to be set on another. The Empyrean Tower, built from the conglomerate resources of the planet's richest wealth, was a gigantic toy, a titillation, a fancy.

But who would know this? The 221st Level housed the finest hospital in the world. The staff read like the Medical Associations' list of Yearly Honors. Level 460 held an Early Cretaceous swamp-forest. Full-scale dinosaurs cropped at archaic vegetation, pterodactyls slipped by on invisible guides, the air held the savage stench of swamp, black ooze, rotting mussels, carrion.

Level 461 enclosed the first human city, Eridu of Sumer, complete with its thirty-foot brick walls, the ziggurat temple to Enlil the Earth god, the palace of the king, the mud huts of the peasants. Level 462 was a Mycenaean Island, lapped by blue salt water. A Minoan temple in an olive grove crowned the height, and a high-beaked galley floated on the water, with sunlight sparkling from bronze shields, glowing from the purple sail.

Level 463 was a landscape from an imaginary fantastic world created by mystic-artist Dyer Lothaire. And Level 509 was a private fairyland, closed to the public, a magic garden inhabited by furtive nymphs.

There were levels for business offices, for dwellings, for laboratories. The fourth level enclosed the world's largest stadium. Levels 320 through 323 housed the University of the

World, and the initial enrollment was forty-two thousand; 255 was the world's vastest library; 328 a vast art gallery.

There were showrooms, retail stores, restaurants, quiet taverns, theaters, telecast studios—a complex of the world society caught, pillared up into the air at the whim of Mervyn Allen. Humanity's lust for lost youth had paid for it. Mervyn Allen sold a commodity beside which every ounce of gold ever mined, every prized possession, every ambition and goal, were like nothing. Eternal life, replenished youth—love, loyalty, decency, honor found them unfair overstrong antagonists.

# CHAPTER IX

## Eyes in the Wall

Briskly Mario alighted from the aircab at the public stage on the 52nd level, the coordination center of the tower. Among the crowds of visitors, tenants, employees, he was inconspicuous. He stepped on a pedestrip to the central shaft, stepped off at the express elevator to Level 600. He entered one of the little cars. The door snapped shut, he felt the surge of acceleration, and almost at once the near-weightlessness of the slowing. The door flicked open, he stepped out on Level 600, two miles in the air.

He was in the lobby of the Paradise Inn, beside which the Atlantic-Empire lobby was mean and constricted. He moved among exquisitely dressed men and women, persons of wealth, dignity, power. Mario was inconspicuous. He might have been a janitor or a maintenance electrician. He walked quietly down a corridor, stopped at last by a door marked *Private*. He thumbed the lock; it opened into a janitor's closet. But the janitors for the 600th level all had other storerooms. No other thumb would spring this lock. In case an officious floor-manager forced the door, it was merely another janitor's closet lost in the confusion.

But it was a very special closet. At the back wall, Mario pushed at a widely separated pair of studs, and the wall fell aside. Mario entered a dark crevice, pushed the wall back into place. Now he was alone—more alone than if he were in the middle of the Sahara. Out in the desert a passing aircraft might spy him. Here in the dead spaces alongside the master columns, among elevator shafts, he was lost from every eye. If he died, no one would find him. In the far, far future,

when the Empyrean Tower was at last pulled down, his
skeleton might be exposed. Until then he had vanished from
the knowledge of man.

He shone his flashlight ahead of him, turned to the central
spinal cord of elevator shafts, tubes like fibers in a tremendous vegetable. Here he found his private elevator, lost
among the others like a man in a crowd. The mechanics who
installed it could not recognize its furtive purpose. It was a
job from a blueprint, part of the day's work, quickly forgotten. To Mario it was a link to Level 900, the Chateau d'If.

He stepped on the tiny platform. The door snapped. Up he
was thrown, up a mile. The car halted, he stepped out. He
was in the Chateau d'If—invisible, a ghost. Unseen, unheard,
power was his. He could strike from nothingness, unsuspect-
ed, unimagined, master of the master of the Chateau d'If.

He breathed the air, exultant, thrilling to his power. This
was the ultimate height of his life. He snapped on his torch,
though there was no need. He knew these passages as if he
had been born among them. The light was a symbol of his
absolute authority. He had no need for skulking. He was in
his private retreat, secure, isolated, remote.

Mario halted, glanced at the wall. At eight-foot intervals
circles of fluorescent paint gleamed brightly. Behind this wall
would be the grand foyer to the Chateau d'If. Mario advanced to one of the fluorescent circles. These he himself had
painted to mark the location of his spy cells. These were little
dull spots hardly bigger than the head of a pin, invisible at
three feet. Mario, in the guise of an electrician, had installed
them himself, with a pair at every location, for binocular
vision.

From his pouch he brought a pair of goggles, clipped a
wire to the terminal contacts of the spy cells, fitted the
goggles over his eyes. Now he saw the interior of the foyer as
clearly as if he were looking through a door.

It was the height of a reception—a house-warming party at
the Chateau d'If. Men, old, young, distinguished or handsome
or merely veneered with the glow of success; women at once
serene and arrogant, the style and show of the planet. Mario
saw jewels, gold, the shine and swing of thousand-colored
fabrics, and at eye-level, the peculiar white-bronze-brown-
black mixture, the color of many heads, many faces—crowd-
color.

Mario recognized some of these people, faces and names
world-known. Artists, administrators, engineers, bon-vivants,

courtesans, philosophers, all thronging the lobby of the Chateau d'If, drawn by the ineffable lure of the unknown, the exciting, the notorious.

There was Mervyn Allen, wearing black. He was as handsome as a primeval sun-hero, tall, confident, easy in his manner, but humble and carefully graceful, combining the offices of proprietor and host.

Thane Paren was nowhere in sight.

Mario moved on. As at 5600 Exmoor, he found a room drenched with amber-white light, golden, crisp as celery, where the broad-leafed plants grew as ardently as in their native humus. The herbarium was empty, the plants suspired numbing perfume for their own delectation.

Mario passed on. He looked into a room bare and undecorated, a workshop, a processing plant. A number of rubber-wheeled tables were docked against a wall, each with its frock of white cloth. A balcony across the room supported an intricate mesh of machinery, black curving arms, shiny metal, glass. Below hung a pair of translucent balls, the pallid blue color of Roquefort cheese. Mario looked closely. These were the golasma cellules.

No one occupied the chamber except a still form on one of the stretchers. The face was partly visible. Mario, suddenly attentive, shifted his vantage point. He saw a heavy blond head, rugged blunt features. He moved to another cell. He was right. It was Janniver, already drugged, ready for the transposition.

Mario gave a long heavy suspiration that shook Ebery's paunch. Ditmar had made it. Zaer, Mario, Breaugh, and now Janniver, lured into this room like sheep the Judas-goat conducts to the abbatoir. Mario bared his teeth in a grimace that was not a smile. A tide of dark rage rose in his mind.

He calmed himself. The grimace softened into the normal loose lines of Ebery's face. Who was blameless, after all? Thane Paren? No. She served Mervyn Allen, the soul in her brother's body. He himself, Roland Mario? He might have killed Mervyn Allen, he might have halted the work of the Chateau d'If by crying loudly enough to the right authorities. He had refrained, from fear of losing his body. Pete Zaer? He might have kept to the spirit of his bargain, warned his friends on the Oxonian Terrace.

All the other victims, who had similarly restrained their rage and sense of obligation to their fellow-men? No, Ditmar was simply a human being, as weak and selfish as any other, and his sins were those of commission rather than those of omission, which characterized the others.

Mario wandered on, peering in apartment, chamber and hall. A blonde girl, young and sweet as an Appalachian gilly-flower, swam nude in Allen's long green-glass pool, then sat on the edge amid a cloud of silver bubbles. Mario cursed the lascivious responses of Ebery's body, passed on. Nowhere did he see Thane Paren.

He returned to the reception hall. The party was breaking up, with Mervyn Allen bowing his guests out, men and women flushed with his food and drink, all cordial, all promising themselves to renew the acquaintance on a later, less conspicuous occasion.

Mario watched till the last had left—the last but one, this an incredibly tall, thin old man, dressed like a fop in pearl-gray and white. His wrists were like corn-stalks, his head was all skull. He leaned across Mervyn Allen's shoulder, a roguish perfumed old dandy, waxed, rouged, pomaded.

Now Allen made a polite inquiry, and the old man nodded, beamed. Allen ushered him into a small side room, an office painted dark gray and green.

The old man sat down, wrote a check. Allen dropped it into the telescreen slot, and the two waited, making small talk. The old man seemed to be pressing for information, while Allen gracefully brushed him aside. The television flickered, flashed an acknowledgment from the bank. Allen rose to his feet. The old man arose. Allen took a deep breath; they stepped into the herbarium. The old man took three steps, tottered. Allen caught him deftly, laid him on a concealed rubber-tired couch, wheeled him forward, out into the laboratory where Janniver lay aready.

Now Mario watched with the most careful of eyes, and into a socket in his goggles he plugged another cord leading to a camera in his pouch. Everything he saw would be recorded permanently.

There was little to see. Allen wheeled Janniver under one of the whey-colored golasma cellules, the old man under another. He turned a dial, kicked at a pedal, flicked a switch, stood back. The entire balcony lowered. The cellules engulfed the two heads, pulsed, changed shape. There was motion on the balcony, wheels turning, the glow of luminescence. The operation appeared self-contained, automatic.

Allen seated himself, lit a cigarette, yawned. Five minutes

passed. The balcony rose, the golasma cellules swung on an axis, the balcony lowered. Another five minutes passed. The balcony raised. Allen stepped forward, threw off the switches.

Allen gave each body an injection from the same hypodermic, rolled the couches into an adjoining room, departed without a backward glance.

Toward the swimming pool, thought Mario. Let him go!

At nine o'clock in Tanagra Square, a cab dropped off a feeble lackluster old man, tall and thin as a slat, who immediately sought a bench.

Mario waited till the old man showed signs of awareness, watched the dawning alarm, the frenzied examination of emaciated hands, the realization of fifty stolen years. Mario approached, led the old man to a cab, took him to his apartment. The morning was a terrible one.

Janniver was asleep, exhausted from terror, grief, hate for his creaking old body. Mario called the Brannan agency, asked for Murris Slade. The short heavy man with the narrow head appeared on the screen, gazed through the layers of ground glass at Mario.

"Hello, Slade," said Mario. "There's a job I want done tonight."

Slade looked at him with a steady wary eye. "Does it get me in trouble?"

"No."

"What's the job?"

"This man you've been watching for me, Roland Mario, do you know where to find him?"

"He's at the Persian Terrace having breakfast with the girl he spent the night with. Her name is Laura Lingtza; she's a dancer at the Vedanta Epic Theater."

"Never mind about that. Get a piece of paper, copy what I'm going to dictate."

"Go ahead, I'm ready."

" 'Meet me at eleven p.m. at the Cambodian Pillar, lobby of Paradise Inn, Level Six Hundred, Empyrean Tower. Important. Come by yourself. Please be on time, as I can spare only a few minutes. Mervyn Allen, Chateau d'If.' "

Mario waited a moment till Slade looked up from his writing. "Type that out," he said. "Hand it to Roland Mario at about nine-thirty tonight."

# CHAPTER X

## New Bodies for Old

Restlessly Mario paced the floor, pudgy hands clasped behind his back. Tonight would see the fruit of a year's racking toil with brain and imagination. Tonight, with luck, he would shed the hateful identity of Ralston Ebery. He thought of Louis Correaos. Poor Louis, and Mario shook his head. What would happen to Louis' Airfarer? And Letya Arnold? Would he go back out into Tanagra Square to lurk and hiss as Ralston Ebery sauntered pompously past?

He called the Aetherian Block, got put through to Louis Correaos. "How's everything, Louis?"

"Going great. We're all tooled up, be producing next week."

"How's Arnold?"

Correaos screwed up his face. "Ebery, you'll think I'm as crazy as Arnold. But he can fly faster than light."

*"What?"*

"Last Thursday night he wandered into the office. He acted mysterious, told me to follow him. I went. He took me up to his observatory—just a window at the sky where he's got a little proton magniscope. He focused it, told me to look. I looked, saw a disk—a dull dark disk about as large as a full moon. 'Pluto,' said Arnold. 'In about ten minutes, there'll be a little white flash on the left-hand side.' 'How do you know?' 'I set off a flare a little over six hours ago. The light should be reaching there about now.'

"I gave him a queer look, but I kept my eye glued on the image, and sure enough—there it was, a little spatter of white light. 'Now watch,' he says, 'there'll be a red one.' And he's right. There's a red light." Correaos shook his big sandy head. "Ebery, I'm convinced. He's got me believing him."

Mario said in a toneless voice, "Put him on, Louis, if you can find him."

After a minute or so Letya Arnold's peaked face peered out of the screen. Mario said leadenly, "Is this true, Arnold? That you're flying faster than light?"

Arnold said peevishly, "Of course it's true, why shouldn't it be true?"

"How did you do it?"

"Just hooked a couple of electron-pushers on to one of

your high-altitude aircars. Nothing else. I just turned on the juice. The hook-up breaks blazing fury out of the universe. There's no acceleration, no momentum, nothing. Just speed, speed, speed, speed. Puts the stars within a few days' run, I've always told you, and you said I was crazy." His face wrenched, gall burnt at his tongue. "I'll never see them, Ebery, and you're to blame. I'm a dead man. I saw Pluto, I wrote my name on the ice, and that's how I'll be known."

He vanished from the screen. Correeos returned. "He's a goner," said Correeos gruffly. "He had a hemorrhage last night. There'll be just one more—his last."

Mario said in a far voice, "Take care of him, Louis. Because tomorrow I'm afraid maybe things will be different."

"What do you mean—different?"

"Ralston Ebery's disposition might suffer a relapse."

"God forbid."

Mario broke the connection, went back to his pacing, but now he paced slower, and his eyes saw nothing of where he walked. . . .

Mario called a bellboy. "See that young man in the tan jacket by the Cambodian Pillar?"

"Yes, sir."

"Give him this note."

"Yes, sir."

Ralston Ebery had put loose flesh on Mario's body. Pouches hung under the eyes, the mouth was loose, wet. Mario sweated in a sudden heat of pure anger. The swine, debauching a sound body, unused to the filth Ebery's brain would invent!

Ebery read the note, looked up and down the lobby. Mario had already gone. Ebery, following the instructions, turned down the corridor toward the air-baths, moving slowly, indecisively.

He came to a door marked *Private*, which stood ajar. He knocked.

"Allen, are you there? What's this all about?"

"Come in," said Mario.

Ebery cautiously shoved his head through the door. Mario yanked him forward, slapped a hand-hypo at Ebery's neck. Ebery struggled, kicked, quivered, relaxed. Mario shut the door.

"Get up," said Mario. Ebery rose to his feet, docile,

glassy-eyed. Mario took him through the back door, up in the elevator, up to Level 900, the Chateau d'If.

"Sit down, don't move," said Mario. Ebery sat like a barnacle.

Mario made a careful reconnaissance. This time of night Mervyn Allen should be through for the day.

Allen was just finishing a transposition. Mario watched as he pushed the two recumbent forms into the outer waiting room, and then he trailed Allen to his living quarters, watched while he shed his clothes, jumped into a silk jerkin, ready for relaxation or sport with his flower-pretty blonde girl.

The coast was clear. Mario returned to where Ebery sat.

"Stand up, and follow me."

Back down the secret corridors inside the ventilation ducts, and now the laboratory was empty. Mario lifted a hasp, pulled back one of the pressed-wood wall panels.

"Go in," he said. "Lie down on that couch." Ebery obeyed.

Mario wheeled him across the room to the racked putty-colored brainmolds, wheeled over another couch for himself. He held his mind in a rigid channel, letting himself think of nothing but the transposition.

He set the dials, kicked in the foot pedal, as Allen had done. Now to climb on the couch, push one more button. He stood looking at the recumbent figure. Now was the time. Act. It was easy; just climb on the couch, reach up, push a button. But Mario stood looking, swaying slightly back and forth.

A slight sound behind him. He whirled. Thane Paren watched him with detached amusement. She made no move to come forward, to flee, to shout for help. She watched with an expression—quizzical, unhuman. Mario wondered, how can beauty be refined to such reckless heights, and still be so cold and friendless? If she were wounded, would she bleed? Now, at this moment, would she run, give the alarm? If she moved, he would kill her.

"Go ahead," said Thane. "What's stopping you? I won't interfere."

Mario had known this somehow. He turned, looked down at his flaccid body. He frowned.

"Don't like its looks?" asked Thane. "It's not how you remember yourself? You're all alike, strutting, boastful animals."

"No," said Mario slowly, "I thought all I lived for was to

get back my body. Now I don't know. I don't think I want it.
I'm Ebery the industrialist. He's Mario, the playboy."

"Ah," said Thane raising her luminous eyebrows, "you like
the money, the power."

Mario laughed, a faint hurt laugh. "You've been with those
ideas too long. They've gone to your head. There's other
things. The stars to explore. The galaxy—a meadow of magnificent jewels. . . . As Ebery, I can leave for the stars next
week. As Mario, I go back to the Oxonian Terrace, play
handball."

She took a step forward. "Are you—"

He said, "Just this last week a physicist burst through
whatever the bindings are that are holding things in. He
made it to Pluto in fifteen minutes. Ebery wouldn't listen to
him. He's so close to dead right now, you couldn't tell the
difference. Ebery would say he's crazy, jerk the whole project.
Because there's no evidence other than the word of two
men."

"So?" asked Thane. "What will you do?"

"I want my body," said Mario slowly. "I hate this pig's
carcass worse than I hate death. But more than that, I want
to go to the stars."

She came forward a little. Her eyes shone like Vega and
Spica on a warm summer night. How could he have ever
thought her cold? She was quick, hot, full-bursting with
verve, passion, imagination. "I want to go too."

"Where is this everybody wants to go?" said a light baritone voice, easy on the surface, yet full of a furious under-
current. Mervyn Allen was swiftly crossing the room. He
swung his great athlete's arms loose from the shoulder, clench-
ing and unclenching his hands. "Where do you want to
go?" He addressed Mario. "Hell, is it? Hell it shall be." He
rammed his fist forward.

Mario lumbered back, then forward again. Ebery's body
was not a fighting machine. It was pulpy, pear-shaped, and in
spite of Mario's ascetic life, the paunch still gurgled, swung
to and fro like a wet sponge. But he fought. He fought with a
red ferocity that matched Allen's strength and speed for a
half-minute. And then his legs were like columns of pith, his
arms could not seem to move. He saw Allen stepping forward, swinging a tremendous massive blow that would crush
his jaw like a cardboard box, jar out, shiver his teeth.

*Crack!* Allen screamed, a wavering falsetto screech, sagged, fell with a gradual slumping motion.

Thane stood looking at the body, holding a pistol.

"That's your brother," gasped Mario, more terrified by Thane's expression than by the fight for life with Allen.

"It's my brother's body. My brother died this morning. Early, at sunrise. Allen had promised he wouldn't let him die, that he would give him a body. . . . And my brother died this morning."

She looked down at the hulk. "When he was young, he was so fine. Now his brain is dead and his body is dead."

She laid the gun on a table "But I've known it would come. I'm sick of it. No more. Now we shall go to the stars. You and I, if you'll take me. What do I care if your body is gross? Your brain is you."

"Allen is dead," said Mario as if in a dream. "There is no one to interfere. The Chateau d'If is ours."

She looked at him doubtfully, lip half-curled. "So?"

"Where is the telescreen?"

The room suddenly seemed full of people. Mario became aware of the fact with surprise. He had noticed nothing; he had been busy. Now he was finished.

Sitting anesthetized side by side were four old men, staring into space with eyes that later would know the sick anguish of youth and life within reach and lost.

Standing across the room, pale, nervous, quiet, stood Zaer, Breaugh, Janniver. And Ralston Ebery's body. But the body spoke with the fast rush of thought that was Letya Arnold's.

And in Letya Arnold's wasted body, not now conscious, dwelt the mind of Ralston Ebery.

Mario walked in his own body, testing the floor with his own feet, swinging his arms, feeling his face. Thane Paren stood watching him with intent eyes, as if she were seeing light, form, color for the first time, as if Roland Mario were the only thing that life could possibly hold for her.

No one else was in the room. Murris Slade, who had lured, bribed, threatened, frightened those now in the room to the Chateau d'If, had not come farther than the foyer.

Mario addressed Janniver, Zaer, Breaugh. "You three, then, you will take the responsibility?"

They turned on him their wide, amazed eyes, still not fully recovered from the relief, the joy of their own lives. "Yes." . . . "Yes." . . . "Yes."

"Some of the transpositions are beyond help. Some are dead or crazy. There is no help for them. But those whom you can return to their own bodies—to them is your responsibility."

"We break the cursed machine into the smallest pieces possible," said Breaugh. "And the Chateau d'If is only something for whispering, something for old men to dream about."

Mario smiled. "Remember the advertisement? 'Jaded? Bored? Try the Chateau d'If.'"

"I am no longer jaded, no longer bored," sighed Zaer.

"We got our money's worth," said Janniver wryly.

Mario frowned. "Where's Ditmar?"

Thane said, "He has an appointment for ten o'clock tomorrow morning. He comes for the new body he has earned."

Breaugh said with quiet satisfaction, "We shall be here to meet him."

"He will be surprised," said Janniver.

"Why not?" asked Zaer. "After all, this is the Chateau d'If."